A Candlelight Ecstasy Romance®

"I NEED A COMMITMENT FROM YOU. SOMETHING I CAN HOLD ON TO," REBECCA SAID URGENTLY.

"I didn't think you were interested in marriage," Jared said, looking cornered.

"It's not marriage I want, it's you—your love, your willingness to stick by our relationship even during the times it's not perfect."

Jared shook his head, and she felt a sinking sensation in her stomach. "I can't promise you that."

"Do you need more time?" she asked.

"Time isn't the problem. I just don't want to make a promise I might not keep."

"So what shall we do," she asked, her voice thick with tears. "Is this the end?"

"You'll have to decide," he said softly. "It's you who want more."

CANDLELIGHT ECSTASY ROMANCES®

TOMORROW AND ALWAYS

Nona Gamel

A CANDLELIGHT ECSTASY ROMANCE®

Published by
Dell Publishing Co., Inc.
1 Dag Hammarskjold Plaza
New York, New York 10017

ISBN: 0-440-18987-X

Printed in the United States of America

First printing—September 1985

To Our Readers:

We have been delighted with your enthusiastic response to Candlelight Ecstasy Romances®, and we thank you for the interest you have shown in this exciting series.

In the upcoming months we will continue to present the distinctive, sensuous love stories you have come to expect only from Ecstasy. We look forward to bringing you many more books from your favorite authors and also the very finest work from new authors of contemporary romantic fiction.

As always, we are striving to present the unique, absorbing love stories that you enjoy most—books that are more than ordinary romance. Your suggestions and comments are always welcome. Please write to us at the address below.

Sincerely,

The Editors
Candlelight Romances
1 Dag Hammarskjold Plaza
New York, New York 10017

CHAPTER ONE

Jared opened the heavy wooden door easily and looked around with a faint frown. Dr. Collins had said this psychologist was very experienced with cases like Meredith's, but this small waiting room looked quite new. There was no one there, and no reception desk, so he walked in, closing the door quietly behind him.

It was a comfortable room, even cozy. The sofa and armchair were upholstered in a floral pattern that contained shades of rose and beige, with a few soft green leaves here and there. The beige carpet was thick and hadn't had much wear.

He sat down in the armchair and leafed through the small stack of magazines on the table next to him. All were quite up to date, but the selection of teenage music and fashion magazines, a few sports magazines, and a newspaper held little appeal for him.

He probably wouldn't be able to concentrate on reading until he felt he was making some progress in helping his sister. He looked around, trying to see the office through Meredith's eyes. Would she feel at ease coming here, and be able to confide her problems to this psychologist? She would love the wildlife photographs on the cream-colored walls, he knew, but the important question was how she would feel about the therapist.

There was a second door in the room, which presumably led to the psychologist's office, and he stared at it, willing it to open. His watch showed that it was exactly 2 o'clock. With any luck this Dr. Simpson would be prompt. Since he'd returned from Nepal the night before last and seen the wraith that his formerly healthy sister had become, he'd been moving as quickly as he could. Every minute of delay seemed dangerous. Furthermore, he had little respect for people who couldn't keep to their schedules, and he wanted very much to approve of this psychologist.

The door clicked, warning him that it was about to open, and he looked up expectantly. "Dr. Simpson?" He rose to his feet and extended his hand, cursing the audible note of amazement that had crept into his voice. Far from being what he had expected, Dr. D. Rebecca Simpson was younger than he, tall, and what he would call interesting-looking. He firmly gripped the rather large hand she offered him and continued to study her heart-shaped face, large eyes, and deep brown hair. She wasn't really pretty, especially with her hair pulled back so tightly, but on the other hand she was appealing in a way he found hard to define.

The hem of her beige dress fell to the middle of her calves, he noted as she walked in front of him to her office, and its matching jacket was long and loose enough to hide her hips completely. It was impossible to learn much about her figure, although her ankles were narrow enough to suit him. With a slight effort he refocused his attention. After all, he wasn't here to find out whether he was attracted to this psychologist but to determine whether Meri should come to her for therapy.

Like her waiting room, Dr. Simpson's office seemed designed to suggest comfort and security. A fine old desk was unobtrusive against one wall, the desk chair pushed tightly against it. Closer to the door were a long curved sofa and three overstuffed chairs, all in soft shades of blue and beige. He hesitated, and she gestured to one of the chairs, sitting down herself at the end of the sofa and picking up a small pad of paper from a square table at her elbow.

They were at right angles, their knees nearly touching, and he used the opportunity to study her more closely. Her skin was very pale and unfreckled, her eyes a light hazel. Honey-colored, he decided. Her hair grew to a small widow's peak on her rather high forehead, which added a dramatic touch to her completely unadorned face.

Her hair was dark and glossy, its red and gold strands glinting and sparkling in the sunlight that shone through the window behind her. It could have been her best feature, if she'd let it fall in loose waves around her face. Perversely, she had pulled it ruthlessly back from her temples and confined it in a gold clip at her neck.

Her ears were small and very slightly pointed at the top, like little elves' ears. And, somewhat unexpectedly, they were decorated with gold studs, the only jewelry she wore. Nature had been generous with her features. Instead of the classic straight lips, thin nose, and oval eyes, she had a wide, soft mouth, eyes that were nearly round, and a nose that flared a bit at the end. Her eyebrows were straight and rather heavy. It was a face he could study for hours.

Her eyebrows twitched slightly as he admired them, and he immediately produced what he hoped was a charming smile.

"I'm sorry. My mind was wandering a little." She wasn't smiling back, so he tried to look apologetic. "Jet lag."

She nodded. Obviously she wasn't convinced, and he could hardly blame her. He'd been looking her

11

over, and in a very conspicuous way. If he'd been less worried or had more time to recuperate from his flight from Nepal, he certainly would have managed a little subtlety.

"You're here to talk to me about your sister?" she asked, tilting her head a little to look at him. Her voice was pleasantly low and had a break that roughened it and made it a delight to listen to.

"Her pediatrician, Dr. Collins, recommended that I talk to you," he began, then paused. He didn't know where to start. He could tell her about the shock he had experienced at the airport, when he'd seen Meri for the first time in two years. He could describe his sister's new frailty, her withdrawn manner, her refusal to eat no matter how long she was forced to sit at the table. He could begin with his mother's four marriages, or describe his and Meri's newest stepfather. He sighed.

"Perhaps it would help if I told you a little about what I do," she said in that fascinating voice, and he nodded.

"I'm a family therapist, and I most often see families that are concerned about an adolescent family member. As a rule, I don't see individual patients. Occasionally I see married couples without their children. I never see children without their parents."

"I see." That gave him pause. It was hard to imagine his mother and her new husband, George, coming in regularly with Meri. They were so determined that she be perfect, so insistent that she present them with a new accomplishment every week. To bring her here would be an admission of failure, a weekly source of embarrassment. And he doubted that either Sybil or George had the strength to commit themselves to such a course.

"What constitutes a family?" he asked. He'd be glad

to come with Meredith. He'd gladly do whatever was necessary to help her get better.

"Everyone living in the same household. Sometimes people living outside the household, if they are very much on everyone's minds. And I do insist that everyone participate."

"Frankly, I don't see how I can get the three of them in here every week—my mother, her fourth husband, and my sister. Getting my sister here will be difficult enough, but in her case I can always use brute force."

He was silent a moment, trying again to picture the three of them in the office. Meredith, thin as a pencil in her school uniform, would be withdrawn at first. His mother would wear a designer suit, and her silver hair would be carefully brushed into intimidating perfection. As always, she would look glamorous and self-assured, and she would try to dominate the discussion from the moment she sat down.

And then there was George, a very square-jawed, very manly, man who would nonetheless echo Sybil's every phrase. Jared shook his head. He'd never be able to persuade George and Sybil to come. After all, there'd been a three-hour argument about his telephone call to Meri's pediatrician, and when Jared had announced his plan to find out more about Dr. Simpson, Sybil had turned red all the way down to her knuckles. Jared didn't have any illusions about his influence over her.

"Exactly why are you concerned about your sister?"

"She's starving herself." He looked closely at her face, expecting shock or disbelief, but she calmly made a note on her pad. "When I saw her two years ago," he went on, "she was a little chubbier than most girls her age. I thought she'd lose the weight when she grew taller. But instead she's shrunk somehow, and turned

13

into a rail." He gestured helplessly in the air. "The pediatrician says she's lost fifteen pounds in the last year. And while that weight loss hasn't harmed her, it's obvious that she has to start eating normally very soon or else she'll have serious health problems."

"Where is your sister's father?"

He shrugged. "He was the husband before last, and I can't say he ever took much interest in Meri. Right now I think he's in Germany."

"Your family seems rather mobile." Her voice was neutral.

He grimaced. "In more ways than one." Thus far marriage had been more of a hobby than a commitment to his mother, and his various stepfathers had all had rather extensive marital histories.

A cloud passed over the sun, darkening the office and removing the highlights from the psychologist's hair. Her skin seemed whiter, her eyes bigger, and he found himself staring at her again. She sat very still, without fidgeting or even changing the expression on her face. It created in him a desire to prod her, to elicit a response.

"Where do we go from here?" he asked.

"Personally, I find family therapy the ideal treatment for anorexia." She stopped, and he nodded impatiently. Of course he knew that his sister's refusal to eat was called anorexia. The question in his mind was not the diagnosis of her problem but the solution to it.

One corner of her mouth lifted slightly. "As a family therapist, I find that most problems are best treated by family therapy."

So she did have a sense of humor, although it was a little subdued.

"If you don't see any hope for family treatment in your sister's case . . ." Her voice was enchanting, each little break or huskiness a wonderful surprise.

"I could bring Meredith myself." He hesitated. "I mean, I'd come with her for treatment. She's my half-sister, after all."

"Do you live in the house with her and your parents?"

He shook his head. "I'm staying there just until the end of the week. I haven't lived at home for years, but Meri and I were always very close."

"You haven't seen her for two years?" The sun was shining again and he couldn't read her expression, but he thought he detected disapproval in her tone.

"I was in Nepal on business," he explained. "If I'd known things were going so badly for her, I would have made an effort to get back sooner. But all I got were glowing letters." He touched his mustache absently. "They didn't send any pictures."

"Nepal." She considered him for a moment. "Did you do any mountain climbing while you were there?"

"I tried one climb." He leaned back into the sofa, suddenly exhausted. "In the end I felt like the grizzly who forgot to hibernate."

Her eyes widened. "Yes?"

"Bear-ly surviving," he muttered. He thought he should just go home and go to bed, not sit around a psychologist's office making terrible puns.

Her nose wrinkled, the corners of her mouth tilted, and he straightened in the chair. Her tiny smile illuminated half the office. She was beautiful, after all.

"That was awful," she told him, and he gave a modest shrug.

"I know."

A companionable silence fell while he admired the curve of her lips. Had he caught a glimpse of a dimple in her cheek? It was hard to be sure. The smile had been so small, so fleeting. Now her face was blank again.

When he thought about it he was surprised that he had actually made a joke, no matter how feeble. He'd hardly been able to smile since that horrible moment at the airport when he'd suddenly recognized the hollow-cheeked girl standing next to his mother. Obviously he was punchy from the time change, but he thought there was something more going on. He genuinely wanted to amuse this woman, wanted to be friends with her. And for some reason he felt relaxed enough to try. Maybe she had some mysterious skill he hadn't noticed, an ability to let people be themselves. And if she did, she was the ideal person to help his sister, who certainly didn't seem to be herself lately.

"I think the best thing for you to do is to take your sister to a colleague of mine. She's also a good friend, and I know you can have every confidence in her. She runs a small therapy group of girls with eating disorders." She walked over to her desk, rummaged in the center drawer, and came back with a small business card.

Dr. Alice Fairweather, he read silently, and couldn't resist. "Not a fair-weather friend, I hope?"

"Oh, dear." She scowled, but then the smile was back, even broader than before. He was entranced, elated by this woman. At the rate he was going he'd have her laughing by nightfall.

"Dr. Collins, the pediatrician, said you were the best." He hesitated, but she didn't fill the silence. "I'd like Meri to come here rather than to go to Dr. Fairweather."

She frowned, and he admired the four small lines that appeared between her eyebrows. "If you think you can persuade her, her mother, and her stepfather to come in, that will be fine. Otherwise I won't be able

16

to see her. And I recommend Alice Fairweather very highly."

She was beautiful, but stubborn. He sighed, shifting his position a little. Obviously he'd have to take Meredith to the other psychologist, just when he'd decided that Dr. Simpson was someone he'd be delighted to see on a regular basis.

He was tired of thinking of her so formally and glanced at the group of diplomas on the wall. *D. Rebecca Simpson,* they all said. Well, that was one way of keeping visitors in their place. He could hardly try calling her *D,* could he?

"Is there anything else I can help you with?" she asked, and he realized that once again he'd let the silence go on too long.

"I was wondering . . ." He hesitated, then took a deep breath and rushed ahead. "Maybe all this is my fault. If I hadn't gone to Nepal—if I hadn't left her for so long—would this still have happened?" He watched her closely, his hands clenched on his thighs.

"You're suggesting that your sister stopped eating because you left her?"

"Is that likely? I never would have gone if I'd thought something like this would happen. She seemed to be so happy before I left. But now I realize she probably depended on me for a lot of things she can't get from her father or stepfather."

"How old is your sister?" Her voice was soft now, infinitely reassuring.

"Thirteen," he answered.

"So she was just entering puberty around the time you left." She smiled. It was a professional, calming smile, not the marvelous, spontaneous glow he'd seen earlier, but it was very nice just the same. "That's a typical age for this kind of problem. On the other hand, it's entirely possible that if you'd stayed, she

17

would have found life less stressful and this wouldn't have happened."

His tension was too great to allow him to remain sitting quietly in the chair. He stood and walked around her to look out the window. The view was hardly exciting. Her office was in one of several medical buildings near the hospital. He could see the parking lot, a grassy field, and a neighboring building. The perfectly blue and clear sky was typical for an early spring day on the San Francisco peninsula.

Oak trees dotted the field, and at the fourth floor of the building next door a bird feeder was surrounded by finches and sparrows. As he began to turn away, he caught a glimpse of movement in the corner of his vision and looked back. Two girls in their early teens were riding their bicycles down the street, their bodies healthy and strong-looking in their blue jeans and hooded sweat tops. *Meri should look like that,* he thought. *She should be out with her friends instead of hiding in her bedroom, alone and miserable.* He rested his hands on the windowsill and closed his eyes briefly against the glare of the sun, aware of its warmth on the side of his face.

He never should have left Meredith. His mother seemed to have little sympathy for her only daughter. She'd been a better mother to him than she was to Meri, but of course that had been over twenty-five years ago, when his father was still alive. Or perhaps she'd been just as she was now, and his father had made up for her deficiencies. Jared had never really thought about it before.

Certainly Sybil seemed almost indifferent to Meri except as a showpiece, something to brag to her friends about. And George. Jared scowled at the window. George thought of little but golf and cars. He was willing enough to criticize his stepdaughter when the opportunity arose, and apparently considered that an adequate contribution to her upbringing.

Jared had known he'd miss Meri: the way she laughed at his jokes, her fierce tennis game, her fine straight brown ponytail which he loved to pull. But for some reason it had never occurred to him that she needed him emotionally, that he was almost like a father to her. Dr. Simpson, of course, had no way of knowing whether he was to blame for Meredith's anorexia. All he could be sure of was that if he had been in California, or anywhere in the United States, he would never have let things go as far as they had. Sybil and George must have been blind, and they still denied that there was any problem beyond what they called Meri's stubbornness.

"I'd guess your sister lives in an upper-middle-class family and attends a good, demanding school." Her voice interrupted his thoughts. "She takes lots of lessons—tennis, ballet, maybe piano. She gets good grades, but they're never good enough to satisfy her or to impress her parents. She always looks nice, has acceptable friends, and never gets into trouble."

He turned around, looking down at her. She had shifted slightly on the sofa in order to see him, and her legs were crossed at the knee. He glanced quickly at the inch of stockinged thigh that was exposed, at the same time moving to take the chair across from her.

"You've described Meredith quite well," he told her.

She shrugged, still looking very capable and professional. "I was showing off a little, but the point is not to waste your energy trying to pin blame. However the situation came about, the only important thing is to remedy it."

"Suppose it did happen because of me," he said. "What should I do now?"

She thought for a moment, drawing something on her pad of paper. "Of course I know very little about your sister. Whether or not your absence has been a problem for her, I think my recommendation would be the same. Don't discuss food with her at all." She made a slicing gesture with one hand. "Stay away from conversations about food and diets, give her all the love and support you can, *and* take her to Alice Fairweather." She laid her pad and pencil on the table as if to end the discussion.

He wasn't ready to leave. He gestured toward her diplomas. "What does the *D* stand for?"

He thought she almost smiled. "Why do you ask?"

Might as well be honest, he decided. "I wanted to call you by your first name, but I can't figure out what it is." He stroked his mustache with one finger. "Diane? Dorothy? Dagmar? Delilah?"

Her head was tilted to one side, and she didn't say anything. She wore that impassive expression, the one he didn't like, on her face again. The least the woman could do was tell him what to call her. Or maybe she was telling him she wanted to be called Dr. Simpson.

"Diabola. Delbert? Diggery? Dasher? Dancer?" She was sitting very still. "I know. Daphne? Dorcas?" He thought for a while, then looked at her.

"My friends call me Rebecca," she said in a rather soft voice, not meeting his eyes.

What did that mean? he wondered. Obviously he couldn't consider himself a friend, since they were barely acquainted.

"And what do your acquaintances call you?"

Her eyebrows lifted a little, and he waited for a smile, but it never came. "I suppose my acquaintances call me Rebecca too. My patients usually call me Dr. Simpson, and I also use their last names."

20

If anything, that had muddied the waters. She was being coy with him. He rubbed his temples.

"May I call you Rebecca?"

Unexpectedly she smiled, and he beamed back in response. "As long as you promise to take your sister to Alice Fairweather," she replied, still smiling.

"May I call you Rebecca and still ask your advice from time to time?"

"I don't want to get in Alice's way. It would be best if you consulted her—assuming your sister becomes her patient, of course."

"Of course." He was crestfallen. What good would it do him to call her Rebecca if he never had an excuse to talk to her again. Obviously she wasn't at all interested in seeing him again. She was probably married, or engaged. He yawned widely, barely managing to cover his mouth. "Excuse me. I just flew back the night before last and I haven't really adjusted yet to the time change."

She nodded, looking at him, and it was very clear she expected him to leave. Perhaps his forty-five minutes had passed; he couldn't be sure. He studied her face, committing it to memory. If she let her hair fall free, or even cut it short, she'd be much softer-looking and more attractive. But her dress was really a straightforward announcement that she wasn't interested in attracting men. It was too bad. With her incredible smile and fascinating voice, she could leave her path strewn with fawning suitors. *If she smiled a little more often,* he qualified quickly. That rather blank, inward look she had now wasn't much of a magnet.

He stood. "Thank you for all your help."

She extended her hand, and he gripped it firmly. "I hope I'll see you again sometime," he said. A weak effort, but the best he could manage. If she'd seemed more available, he would have asked if he could take her to dinner sometime.

"I'd be interested to hear how your sister progresses," she said, and his spirits lifted. At least she'd given him an excuse to talk to her again. He let her hand go a little reluctantly and turned to leave.

"You can use this door to leave," she told him, waving toward an inconspicuous closed door in the corner near the desk. "That way no one has to worry about embarrassing encounters in the waiting room."

"I see." He stepped around her, wanting to take her hand again. "Does this make people feel as if they're sneaking away after an illicit rendezvous?" he asked. "Or is it just me?"

She was silent for a moment, as if frozen still, and then her sudden smile made him want to declare a holiday. "You're the first person who's said that," she said, still radiant. "It certainly had never occurred to me."

He shrugged, feeling a little awkward. She hadn't stopped smiling, and he waited in the doorway, watching her. Under no circumstances would he walk away from such a beautiful face. If she wanted him out, she'd have to turn down her voltage a little. Of course, she seemed to have no idea at all of what her smile could do to a man, which made her all the more enchanting, he observed.

Slowly her face relaxed, resuming what he supposed was her normal expression. It was as if she'd turned the lights out. Might as well go home and call Dr. Fairweather. Maybe he could take Meri in tomorrow.

"Good-bye," he said, turning away quickly.

He walked out of her office and down the blue-carpeted hall to the elevator. He couldn't say that he'd accomplished much, but he wasn't at all sorry Dr. Collins had given him Rebecca's name. The elevator stopped in the lobby, and he walked out to the parking lot, where he looked up at the windows on the fourth floor of the building. A quick movement at one of the windows caught his eye.

Maybe that had been her, although somehow he doubted it. He glanced up again and saw nothing. With a shrug he walked to his car and unlocked the door. She might not be interested in him—or in any man at all—but one way or another he fully intended to see Dr. D. Rebecca Simpson at least one more time.

CHAPTER TWO

Rebecca was standing at the window when Jared Wells appeared in the parking lot, but she stepped back quickly when she saw him turn and look up. Despite her retreat, she thought their eyes might have met. How ridiculous, to be afraid that he might see her. She often looked out her window while she mentally prepared herself to see her next patients. Why should she suddenly feel as if she'd been caught in an embarrassing act?

She glanced at her watch, then sat down at her old mahogany desk. It had belonged to a good friend, and after Rebecca had first inherited it, the desk had occupied a place of honor in her apartment. It never saw much use there, since even back then she had spent most of her time at work. So when she started her own practice, she had had it moved to her office.

It was a fine old piece of furniture that had been lovingly cared for by Rebecca's friend for over fifty years. The desktop had collected a few faint scratches, but it had a soft glow that told of many polishings. At times it was like having a friend in the office, a familiar person to greet on Mondays. She enjoyed being on her own, but occasionally she missed the camaraderie of the clinic.

She ran her hand lightly over its surface, then tilted back her chair to face the bland acoustical tiles of the ceiling. She still had several minutes to herself before her next appointment. A frown creased her forehead as she realized she'd forgotten to tell Jared Wells that she never charged for an initial consultation. Fortunately, money didn't appear to be a concern for him, so he wouldn't be worried about her fee. His gray suit had been exquisitely tailored of what looked like pure lightweight wool, and his shirt and tie had been equally handsome and expensive-looking. *A man who dressed like that was probably used to spending money without much thought.*

Only rarely did a man like him appear in her office. Somehow, with his elegant appearance and dreadful jokes, he'd aroused her personal interest as well as her professional concern for his sister. With a brother like him, the girl would soon be in capable hands, if Rebecca was any judge of character, so she wasn't needlessly distressed by Jared's story. He was not a man to ignore problems, hoping they'd go away. Neither would he sit by passively and watch them grow worse. Of course, his two-year absence gave him a perspective that his mother and stepfather obviously didn't share. His reunion with his family had obviously been a shock to him.

To be honest, she had found him quite good-looking, although his curly brown hair was a little too long. And she had never liked mustaches. His nose was large and slightly hooked, but it was his dark eyes and bushy eyebrows that dominated his face and lent him an air of gentleness that was probably deceptive. He was self-confident and perhaps successful, possibly too accustomed to getting his own way. She didn't really see him as the much-indulged child of wealthy parents, but with his unusual height and rather muscular build, he'd easily have dominated his peers. He had towered over her, and she was five foot eight in her bare feet. She'd guess him to be at least six-three.

It had been a long time since she'd met a man she felt drawn to, a man who made her smile. And now, having referred him to Alice, she'd probably never see him again. Maybe he'd call sometime to discuss his sister, but it seemed unlikely. The leap from a professional to a personal relationship was a long one, and for that reason alone she shouldn't hope to see him again. She prided herself on her realism, which meant putting Jared Wells out of her mind for good.

In any case, she didn't really have room in her life for a man. She was just too busy right now with her new practice to dedicate the time and emotional energy to a relationship.

A small light on her desk flashed red, signaling that the waiting room door had been opened. Checking her watch, she locked Meredith Larsen's folder in her cabinet and turned to greet her next patients, a ten-year-old shoplifter, his supercilious older sister, and their parents.

Six hours later she locked her office door behind her and squared her sagging shoulders. She had started seeing patients at noon and worked straight through until nine, without taking a break for dinner. Since relatively few of her patients were able to schedule appointments during working hours, the lunch and evening hours were her busiest times. She had managed a quick snack between patients, which was fortunate, because by now she was almost too tired to eat and certainly too tired to cook.

She took the elevator to the basement garage and climbed into her white Peugeot, leaning back happily in the black leather seat once she heard the rumble of the diesel engine. It was wonderful to be able to allow herself such luxuries after years of penny-pinching. Someone like Jared Wells, who probably drove a Porsche or a Mercedes, would never enjoy his car half as much as she did hers.

After a half-hour drive through lightly traveled streets, she pulled into the main driveway of her San Francisco condominium complex. Commuting between a high-rise office building and this circle of town houses every day sometimes made her a little sad, as if something were missing from her life. Maybe at heart she longed for the lawns and trees of suburbia. She'd decided against it because she spent so much time at her office. Why worry about cutting and pruning and watering greenery she'd rarely have a chance to enjoy? Of course her cats, Ferdinand and Isabella, might enjoy a yard, but they were much better off indoors, protected from speeding cars and marauding dogs.

She flicked the button to roll her car window down and inserted her plastic card into the slot in the black iron gate. The gate whirred open, and after she retrieved her card, she drove carefully around the circular driveway to her garage. The garage door rose obediently as she pressed the transmitter, and she parked her car in the empty space.

"Rebecca!" It was Madeleine, standing right under the garage door.

"Madeleine, someday I won't hear you and that door will come down on top of you." Rebecca scowled mockingly as she approached her friend. "Now that you're seven months pregnant, I'd think you'd be more careful."

Madeleine laughed. "I can still dodge a garage door. Come and have pizza with us. Cal just got back from the clinic, and we'll be eating in about twenty minutes."

"I'd love some pizza. Just let me change and feed

27

the cats, and I'll be right over." Rebecca walked back through her garage and unlocked the kitchen door. As she switched on the ceiling light, she experienced the same sense of shock she had felt each evening since the paint job had been completed three weeks ago. The change of color from a rather sickening hospital green to stark white with gleaming copper pots and pans hanging on the kitchen walls still made her feel a little as if she'd walked into someone else's rather fancy apartment.

The other changes she'd made were less dramatic, and for the most part she was happy with the redecoration she'd undertaken. Her favorite room, however, was still her pale blue study, shabby and disorganized though it was.

The cats appeared immediately, winding around her ankles and purring. Rebecca laughed as she gave each glossy back one stroke. "I'm not fooled for a minute. You two want dinner, not affection." She opened a can of cat food, spooned it into two dishes, and watched with amusement as the cats inspected the dishes to make sure that each had been given the same dinner.

Ferdinand, a large tortoiseshell-colored cat with ragged ears, had been a stray abandoned near the apartment she had rented several years back. She had taken him in, then realized that he was lonely in the apartment while she was at work. She had found Isabella, a shiny coal-black mischief-maker, at the animal shelter. Now she enjoyed them both and was happy knowing they kept each other entertained during the many hours she spent at her office.

She ran up the carpeted stairs to her pale yellow bedroom and changed quickly into a pair of jeans and a beige cotton sweater. She slipped on a comfortable old pair of loafers and went back down to the kitchen and took a bottle of red wine out of the cupboard. She was a terrible cook, and rather than do Cal and Madeleine the disservice of offering them a dinner that she had prepared, she more often tried to contribute something to each meal she ate at their house. Madeleine wasn't drinking wine now, of course, but Cal would enjoy it.

"Be good," she called to the cats, now curled up on the sofa, and walked quickly through her garage and across a tiny lawn to her friends' house.

Cal stood framed in the doorway, his straight black hair gleaming under the porch light, and Rebecca kissed him lightly on the cheek before she handed him the bottle of wine.

She and Cal had been graduate students together, and both had gotten their first jobs at the mental health clinic where Cal still worked part-time. By the time Cal married Madeleine, Rebecca was a close friend of both, and she saw one or both of them several times a week.

Madeleine was in the kitchen setting the table, and soon all three were sitting around the painted wooden table, each with a large slice of pizza.

"I was talking to Ed Blake today," Cal told Rebecca, having silently devoured two slices of pizza. "He asked about you."

"Cal!" Madeleine was a long-haired Scandinavian blonde whose fair skin reddened under the slightest emotional stress. Now she was as pink as a lobster. Rebecca deliberately occupied herself with her wine. "That's right, Rebecca, just ignore him," Madeleine said. "He's never had any tact."

Cal slapped the table with one hand. "That's completely untrue. I can be the soul of tact when it's called for. But Rebecca and I are old friends, and I think this is a case when plain speaking is more important than social conventions."

29

Madeleine's color was still high, and Rebecca saw that she wasn't about to let Cal pursue the topic. "Friendship isn't a license to make people uncomfortable. You should leave Rebecca alone about Ed Blake."

"Why?" Cal leaned back, balancing precariously on two legs of his chair. "Ed's settled down now, and I think he's finally ready for a serious relationship. And Rebecca is still sitting home alone every Saturday night, so—"

"Stop it!" Now Madeleine's cheeks were like two beets, and Rebecca swallowed miserably. It was time she entered the discussion instead of passively allowing Madeleine to intercept Cal's remarks.

"Right now," she said, "I wouldn't have Ed back if he proposed marriage to me on bended knee. The whole thing was just infatuation on my part, because I was so naive. I'm better off without him. So if he asks about me again, tell him I'm fine, and then change the subject, okay?"

"Rebecca, you know that recently divorced men are inclined to sow some wild oats. But I'm sure Ed always appreciated your good qualities." With the air of having said everything that needed to be said, Cal took the last bite of his pizza.

Giving a light sigh, Madeleine stood, both hands pressing into the small of her back. "I need a more comfortable chair," she said. "So if we're all finished, let's move into the other room."

"I'll put the dishes in the dishwasher," Rebecca said quickly. Cal meant well, but the conversation had been more painful to her than he could have known. Her love affair with Ed Blake had been the very first of her life, and by now she thought it might well be the last. Since she was in practice by herself, she certainly didn't meet any eligible men at work. Usually she was so caught up in her patients and their problems, she hardly even felt the need for an intimate relationship. Of course, despite what she'd said to Cal, she still thought about Ed more often than she should, still wondered why she hadn't been able to hold his interest. Sometimes, after a particularly eventful day, she found herself looking forward to telling Ed all about it until she remembered that she wouldn't be talking to him that evening, or ever.

She rinsed the last blue-flowered dish and closed the dishwasher. Surely by now Madeleine would have managed to interest Cal in a new topic of conversation. She walked into the dining room, which was empty and dark. Cal and Madeleine had just bought their condominium, using all their savings, and many of the rooms were still unfurnished.

"Well, it's not as if she goes to parties every evening," Cal was saying as Rebecca paused at the arched entrance to the living room. "How does she expect to meet anyone new, holed up in her office day and night?"

Madeleine was sitting on a dark blue corduroy sofa, surrounded by a collection of small pillows in various bright colors. "Maybe she doesn't want to meet anyone right now. Why don't we just drop the subject before she comes back?" Her cheeks were still pink, Rebecca saw. They had obviously continued talking about her and Ed while she was in the kitchen.

As usual, Cal was persistent. "We could have Ed over to dinner, and then invite Rebecca too. Without telling her he'd be there."

"That's the worst idea I've heard all day," Madeleine said flatly. "Where did this matchmaking urge of yours come from, anyway?"

"I inherited it from my mother—who, if you'll remember, introduced me to you."

Rebecca stepped out of the dark room and forced a smile. "Everything's neat and tidy in the kitchen."

Madeleine smiled. "You're an angel. If Cal can manage to be inoffensive for a few minutes, why don't you stay and chat?"

Cal stood up. "I'll do even better. I'll go and make some tea, and you two can talk about whatever you like." He looked at his wife. "Maybe you can talk some sense into Rebecca."

"I don't ever want to see Ed again," Rebecca whispered as soon as he was out of the room. "Promise me you won't try to get us together."

Madeleine settled more comfortably into the multicolored sofa cushions. "Don't worry." She twisted the plain gold wedding ring on her finger. "Ed was never good enough for you, and I know it even if Cal doesn't. It's time to forget about him." She looked at Rebecca closely, her pale blue eyes serious. "One way to get over the end of a love affair is to start a new one, you know. And it's been a year, maybe longer. Have you met anyone at all interesting lately?"

Rebecca hesitated. She was very close to Madeleine, but she'd never developed the habit of confiding in anyone. And in this case there was ridiculously little to tell.

"I did meet someone today, the brother of a potential patient. But I'm sure nothing will ever come of it."

"Well, at least it shows you're still alive, if you're beginning to notice men again. Did he seem interested in you?"

Rebecca tucked a stray lock of hair behind her ear. "He's only interested in me as a psychologist, not as a woman. Which is as it should be."

"But you wouldn't mind if his interest turned out to be more personal?" Madeleine's elfin grin always cheered Rebecca up, and she gave a small smile in return.

"I don't know. If his family became my patients, a personal relationship with him would cause a problem."

"Well, tell me what he's like, anyway."

Rebecca paused. "I don't really know," she said eventually. "I don't know what he does for a living, what his interests are, anything like that. He has a younger sister he's very fond of, he likes to make puns, and he just got back from Nepal, where he was living for a couple of years for business reasons."

"Nepal!" Madeleine stood and walked to a stack of newspapers on an end table. "I read some sort of local-boy-makes-good thing in the business section today. I wonder if it had anything to do with him."

Silence fell, broken only by the rustle of newspaper pages, and for some reason Rebecca found herself waiting impatiently for Madeleine to find the article. It might very well be about Jared Wells. After all, how many people had business in Nepal?

"Here." With a final flap Madeleine folded back a section of the paper to display an article entitled "A Unique Location for a New Software Firm." The article was accompanied by a small photograph of Jared sitting with several other men around a low table. Rebecca felt a faint thrill in her chest. "That's him—Jared Wells."

Madeleine peered at the picture while Rebecca skimmed the article. So he and a partner had started a small company in Nepal.

Madeleine sat back down on the sofa and pushed her hair back over her shoulders. "He must be very interesting."

"I suppose." Rebecca was suddenly reluctant to discuss him any further, knowing she was only building

33

up false expectations in both Madeleine and herself. "He didn't talk much about himself, since he was consulting me professionally."

Madeleine nodded, sensing that Rebecca wouldn't reveal any more about the visit, and Cal appeared, balancing three mugs of tea on a painted Mexican tray. "I hope I stayed in the kitchen long enough to suit you," he said, carefully setting down the tray. He looked at Rebecca critically. "Rebecca, I have this fantasy that one day you'll go completely wild—permed hair, skintight pants, a see-through blouse, and sandals with three-inch heels—and knock this city on its ear."

Rebecca shook her head, but Madeleine studied her thoughtfully. "Is there a wild woman inside you? You're the only one who knows."

Rebecca twirled a stray lock of hair around her index finger. "I was more rambunctious as a child—up through my first year of high school. In fact, I was in trouble all the time. I was suspended twice, and nearly expelled."

"It's hard to imagine." Madeleine stirred three spoonfuls of sugar into her tea. "What subdued you?"

Rebecca laughed. "A teacher packed me off to the school psychologist, and that was the first time an adult ever took me seriously. She was like a surrogate mother to me, a very important person in my life. I'm sure it was because of her that I decided to go into psychology. And she encouraged me in that, helped me learn to devote myself to a goal instead of expending my energy on mischief."

"And the rest is history," Cal added. "Is the school psychologist the friend who died a few years back and left you her desk and all her books?"

Rebecca nodded. "Marian Blanchard. She's the one who talked me out of wild hairdos and tight pants, all-night parties—all those wonderful things."

Cal sighed. "What a pity."

Madeleine stood up awkwardly to rearrange several pillows behind her. "I think I'll get a permanent after the baby's born. And buy some new clothes." She gave her husband a sidelong look.

Rebecca grinned. "Now that you know Cal's tastes, there's nothing to stop you. I'll be glad to baby-sit while you're knocking the city on its ear. In fact, I'll baby-sit while you shop for the see-through blouse."

"It's a deal."

Rebecca carried her empty cup to the kitchen and turned to find Madeleine close behind her. "Let me know if there are any developments with Jared Wells."

Rebecca shrugged. "I'm afraid there won't be much to tell."

She said good night to Cal and crossed back to her garage. It would be nice if she could believe that she would have a reason to talk to Madeleine about Jared again. She could easily imagine describing dates with him, her feelings about him . . . except for one thing. Her imagination wasn't fertile enough to suggest how all these things would come about, when there was no reason to expect that they would ever see each other again. Clearly he couldn't call and ask her for a date on the basis of one consultation in her office. He seemed much too sensible for that.

It was a pity, she thought as she climbed the tan carpeted stairs to her bedroom. She'd never before been so immediately attracted to a man. The sunny yellow walls and shutters of her bedroom and the soft rainbow shades of the bedspread cheered her a little, and she resolved to put her hopeless interest in Jared out of her mind.

Three weeks later she was replacing some folders in her filing cabinet when she came across Meredith Larsen's file. She hoped by now the girl was seeing Alice Fairweather regularly. It would be a pity if her problem had gone untreated. The prognosis was so much better when therapy was begun early. She closed the drawer and hesitated. She was tempted to call Alice to see if Jared Wells had gotten in touch with her.

Better leave things alone, she decided. She had patients of her own to tend to. And in this case it was hard to be sure her interest really lay in Meredith and not in her attractive older brother. Rebecca's thoughts had strayed to Jared Wells several times over the past weeks. She thought he probably would have called her if his sister had refused treatment altogether. It was most likely that she was doing fine in Alice's little group of anorexic girls, and that Rebecca would never see Jared Wells again.

With a tiny grimace she finished refiling the folders she had stacked on her lap and pulled out the folder of a family she expected to see that evening. The teenage son had developed ingenious methods of sneaking out of the house at night, to the point that his parents had installed double deadbolt locks on all the doors and bars on their upstairs windows.

Most recently, according to a frantic telephone call she had received earlier in the week, the boy had crawled downstairs and out the kitchen window while his parents watched television in the next room. Rebecca couldn't help admiring his determination, but she'd have to find a way to stop the war between him and his parents before they decided to put an electrified fence around their property.

She stood, giving her desk an affectionate pat. She'd come a long way. In the year she'd been in practice by herself, she'd been surprised and gratified by the number of patients she'd treated. Marian would have been proud of her. The work wasn't as glamorous as she'd once thought, but it was much more fulfilling than she'd expected. Although her heavy caseload hadn't meant a corresponding increase in her income, since she saw many patients at reduced rates, she still had more money than she'd ever dreamed of. She looked down suddenly, plucking at her brown checked dress a little critically. As soon as she found the time, she'd go shopping and buy some new clothes. They couldn't be flamboyant or even very fashionable, because that might overwhelm some of her patients. But it might be fun to look just a little more sophisticated . . . a little more attractive. Vowing to go on a shopping spree as soon as possible, she opened the door to her waiting room and smiled at the nervous family just coming in the outer door.

Two days later the red light flashed on her desk, and Rebecca glanced at her watch. Three o'clock, and she didn't have any appointments scheduled until 4:30. Just to be safe, she should probably get into the habit of locking the outer door when she wasn't expecting anyone. She stood, brushing down her new brown tweed skirt, and opened the door to the waiting room.

His head was bent and turned away from her while he placed a newspaper in his briefcase, but she recognized him immediately and felt her face grow warm.

"I'm sorry to drop in like this, but I was in the neighborhood and took the chance you'd be free. Then when I got here I realized if I knocked to announce my presence, I might disturb a patient. I was anticipating a long siege."

"I have a light that flashes when the door opens," she explained, suddenly feeling awkward. Was his spontaneous visit a social or a business call? Ever since she'd met him, she'd looked forward to seeing him again but had never really expected it to happen.

"Why don't you come into my office," she said, making every effort to regain her composure.

"Fine."

He stood, and she noticed for the first time that he was casually dressed in new-looking jeans and a brown sweater. His sporty clothes made him seem more approachable, somehow. His sweater looked very soft, and she resisted an impulse to touch his sleeve.

They sat down in the same places where they'd sat during Jared's first visit: he in the armchair and she on the sofa. It had been almost a month since she'd seen him, she realized, but somehow it seemed as if only a few days had passed.

"I never received a bill for my consultation with you, so I came to settle accounts." He reached into his briefcase and produced a checkbook, apparently oblivious to the fact that she was shaking her head.

"There's no fee for an initial consultation," Rebecca replied. She didn't believe that this was the only reason he'd stopped by. She certainly hoped it wasn't. Surely he could have asked his secretary to call and inquire about the bill.

"I hope Meredith is seeing Dr. Fairweather," she said.

"Yes, and that was something I wanted to talk to you about. But I can't take up your time for free."

"I make my own decisions about charges and I never charge for consultations," she insisted.

He smiled. "Then perhaps I can take you out to dinner some evening and we can discuss the situation then."

Her pulse fluttered briefly and she looked away from him. "Unfortunately, I'm busy most evenings." A moment after she'd spoken the words she regretted them. Why was she putting him off? She didn't understand why she felt nervous, almost afraid of him. She looked down at her new skirt, which had slits on each side. Was it too revealing, or was it the kind of skirt a man like Jared Wells found attractive on a woman?

He didn't seem perturbed by her evasion. "Are your evenings taken up for business or social reasons?"

She almost sighed. It would have been nice to be able to say that she led a very active social life. "I see patients in the evenings," she told him.

"Well," he said, flashing a winning smile, "what about Sunday evening, then, or do you have to get up early Monday morning?"

"Sunday evening would be fine," she told him.

"Have you been to Gaylord's?"

"No, I haven't. It's an Indian restaurant, isn't it?" Her voice was soft and hesitant. If she knew him a little better, she'd feel more comfortable. As it was, he'd never guess how pleased she was at the prospect of seeing him again.

"Yes, one of my favorites," Jared replied, studying her boldly. Her whole body had taken on that unnatural calm he remembered from their first meeting, and her face was quite expressionless, although it had more color than he remembered. Her clothes seemed more feminine this time too.

The tweed skirt she was wearing fitted her hips nicely, and the slits at the sides revealed attractively shaped knees. Her tailored white blouse was tucked in neatly at the waist, modestly showing the curve of her high, round breasts. He was thankful that she wasn't wearing one of those silly ties around her neck. It was a mystery to him why some women had adopted that rather ridiculous male fashion. Her hair was still pulled back austerely in the style of a nineteenth-century governess, but he was actually growing to like it on her.

He wanted to make her smile again. That was why

he had stopped by instead of picking up the telephone. Her smile had stayed with him, the memory of it causing him to beam at the most unexpected and inappropriate moments. So as soon as he'd thought it at all plausible, he'd used the excuse of the bill to see her at least once more and find out exactly how the land lay. But now, even though she'd agreed to have dinner with him, she seemed so remote. "Write down your address for me, and I'll pick you up at six-thirty," he said. "And here's my card, so you can let me know if your plans change."

She scribbled quickly and handed him a small piece of paper. "There's a phone at the gate. Call me and I'll buzz you in," she said.

He glanced quickly at the paper. "So you live in the city and work in the suburbs. That's the reverse of what most people do."

She shrugged one shoulder. "I grew up in a small valley town, so living in the city still seems very glamorous to me. And the commute is easy, since everyone's going the other way."

He nodded. "I lived in San Francisco for a time myself, when I was younger." He glanced again at the address. "But not in such an opulent neighborhood."

Rebecca shook her head. "The truth is, I live in a little bunch of town houses hidden among all the sixteen-bedroom four-story homes. And I love it there. I take long walks, admiring the stone lions and marble steps and the fountains in the gardens. Sometimes I even pretend I'm a European millionaire."

And there it was again, like a splash of sunlight, a smile every bit as entrancing as he'd remembered. He smiled back, wanting suddenly to squeeze her shoulders or touch her hand, somehow to extend the contact he sensed between them. But her smile was fading, and any minute now she'd tell him a patient was due to arrive.

Standing up, he raised his hand in a small wave. "I'll look forward to seeing you Sunday."

She nodded. "I'll be interested to hear about your sister. I've often wondered how she's doing."

He left feeling vaguely dissatisfied. It had been a mistake to use Meri as an excuse to see Rebecca Simpson on Sunday. Maybe he should have told her he just wanted to sit across a table from her and watch her smile. Instead he had to live with her idea that he was buying her dinner as a way of repaying her for her professional advice. He wondered if she would have accepted an invitation that was strictly social rather than professional.

He punched the elevator button. This seemed to be his day for making a mess of things. He'd had his share of love affairs over the years, although an impartial observer today would have wondered how he'd managed it. Next Sunday he'd have to put things on a more personal basis and make sure Rebecca understood that he wanted to get to know her and not just to obtain her advice about Meredith. As he walked out into the sunshine, he glanced up at her window but didn't see her there.

Stunned, Rebecca sat at her desk. The man had actually come back, and she was going to have dinner with him! She must have made quite an impression on him the first time they'd met, although it was hard to imagine how. She hadn't said anything that was startling or provocative. And it certainly couldn't be her looks that had drawn him back to her. She had often heard that men loved a good listener. Was this perhaps the source of her attractiveness to Jared Wells?

41

CHAPTER THREE

Rebecca looked in the full-length mirror on her closet door and sighed. The dress was all right, she supposed, but she almost wished she had found something new to wear. This same old wheat-colored silk dress had served at wedding receptions, Christmas parties, and even on a few dates with Ed. It went well with her coloring; in fact, there was nothing wrong with it at all. But she was a little tired of it. Still, it would do well enough for a semi-business dinner.

She felt the soft brush of Ferdinand's fur as he twined around her legs, and she absently stroked his tail while she turned to look at the clock on the bedside stand. Jared wouldn't arrive for at least a half-hour. Now that she was dressed, she had lots of time to fix her hair and straighten the living room. She got her white wool jacket out of the closet and went downstairs.

The Sunday paper was spread out all over the floor, and she began to pick it up, marveling at Isabella's ability to sit so firmly on the entertainment section. Ignoring the cat's heartrending complaints about having been dislodged, she stacked the papers neatly in the garage and washed her hands. There was still time to spare. Getting ready early usually meant she was nervous about what lay ahead, but this evening she felt quite calm. Even from the brief time she'd spent with Jared, she knew that the evening would be pleasant.

She sat down at the kitchen table and leafed through a psychiatry journal she had brought home from work. There was an article on eating disorders she had been intending to read, and the date with Jared had brought it to mind. It was unlikely that there'd be much new in the article that could help his sister, but there was always a chance. She was reading the last page, absently stroking Isabella's head to keep her from getting in the way, when her phone rang.

"I'm here," Jared said when she answered, and she felt her heartbeat speed up. "I'm a little early."

"I'll buzz open the gate," she answered.

She pressed the button that would admit his car, wondering at the surge of adrenaline she had felt when she heard his voice. It had come partly from surprise, since she had thought if anything he would be a little late, living so far away. But there was also a tingle of anticipation and a slight fear that when she saw him she'd be disappointed. She closed the journal, marking her place with a paper napkin, and opened the door.

Jared was just coming up the steps. He'd gotten a haircut, she saw right away, and he was holding a bouquet of flowers wrapped in green paper. No one had ever brought her flowers before. She accepted them a little awkwardly, thanking him as he stepped inside and looked around the living room.

"I'll put these in some water," she said. "Sit down if you like, or feel free to look around."

"I'll come into the kitchen with you," he said, "unless you object. If you have a sink full of dirty pots and pans you don't want me to see, just say so."

Rebecca laughed, suddenly feeling relaxed. "The extent of my cooking is popping frozen dinners into the microwave, so I never have dirty pots and pans. In fact, I hardly own any, dirty or clean."

The bouquet was a mixture of spring flowers, and she bent her head to sniff them. By some amazing coincidence she actually owned a flared white vase of the correct size, and she trimmed the flowers and began arranging them just as if she'd been doing it all her life.

He was silent, watching, and she felt his eyes on her. "You look very nice tonight," he said, and she glanced at him.

"Thank you."

"First dates always terrify me a little. So often I find myself having dinner with a stranger, not at all the person I thought I'd be with. But you seem just as I remembered you."

What are you saying he admonished himself. He had put his foot in his mouth again. No wonder she was looking at him so strangely. Here she was all dressed up in a beautiful yellow dress, and he was saying she looked the same as she had in her office. What was it about her that made him lose his usual cool? It must be her wonderful laugh. It was like wine, that rich husky voice laughing, her face brightening. It all went to his head, exhilarating him dangerously and tempting him to act foolish in order to hear it again.

"Would you like a drink?" she asked.

He nodded. "A small Scotch, if you have any."

"Why don't you have a seat in the living room. I'll bring our drinks in there in a minute."

Her living room was striking, decorated in colors that would look good on her. He sat down on a long, low cinnamon-colored corduroy sofa, pushing aside several pale gold cushions.

The sandstone walls were a nice touch, he thought, and he liked the medieval hunting tapestry on the adjacent wall. Its faded red and pale amber colors blended perfectly with the room's modern furniture. He stood again to look at the oil painting over the sofa, a stark forest scene of bare, angular tree branches hung with ice crystals and silhouetted against a dark sky.

Rebecca set the drinks on a tabletop of amber and rose-toned marble and sat down across from him in a low modern chair. Her eyes seemed very large as she looked at him, her face rather pale in the artificial light.

"To a pleasant evening," he said, raising his glass.

She smiled, and their eyes met. The evening was going to be more than just pleasant, he knew. She didn't say anything but leaned back a little farther in her chair, putting her glass down on the wooden arm. The light from one of the brass lamps fell on her hair, making it glint bright red and gold against the muted colors of the tapestry.

"Where did you get that?" he asked, gesturing at the wall hanging.

She turned as if to remind herself. "One of my patients at the clinic gave it to me. That's how I got the other one too."

"They're very unusual, and they suit this room very well."

A little more color came into her cheeks. "You like them?"

"Yes, I like all I've seen of your place."

She nodded, as if confirming something privately to herself. "I'm glad."

Their glasses were empty. "Shall we go?" he asked.

He loved the way she stood, all in one motion from the hips, instead of launching herself with her arms. She picked up a white jacket and he took it from her, standing near enough to be aware of her subtle perfume, a light, spicy scent that didn't cloy. Standing behind her with the jacket, he had to fight down an impulse to stroke the fine dark hairs along the side of her neck, to kiss the hollow under her ear.

She slid her arms into the jacket sleeves and turned to face him. In the shoes she was wearing she was nearly as tall as he, their eyes almost on a level.

"I've been looking forward to this dinner," he said, his voice sounding a little hoarse to his ears. "And I wanted to tell you, just to set the record straight, I didn't invite you out to consult you about my sister."

"Oh?" Rebecca tried desperately to think of a more intelligent response.

"I wanted to get to know you better," he said, and her heart gave a rather unpleasant thump. She was always tongue-tied at moments like this. She hadn't had enough experience to know how to respond, probably. If she'd dated more after high school, presumably she'd have developed automatic responses to remarks like these.

"Well, I've been looking forward to seeing you, too," she said finally as she opened the front door, then stopped on the doorstep. "Look at the moon!" It was an unusually clear night, and she pointed at the tiny sliver of moon overhead. "That's much nicer than a full moon."

He laughed. "I already guessed that you have rather unconventional tastes."

She'd never heard him laugh before. It was a nice, comfortable sound.

"*This* is your car?" She could have kicked herself. Obviously it was his car, since one would hardly borrow or rent such a vehicle, and he undoubtedly would misinterpret her amazement as dismay that she wasn't being taken out in something flashier. It was an ancient black Volvo, high and turtlelike. From what she could see in the dark it was in immaculate condition, its paint gleaming in the light from her porch.

"I had you pegged as a Mercedes or Porsche type," she explained once they were seated inside.

"That just shows you the folly of stereotypes. This was my first car," he went on, waiting a moment before he started the engine. "I bought it used and abused and fixed it up. It's never let me down, so I've never been able to bring myself to sell it." He patted the wooden dashboard fondly, and Rebecca smiled to herself.

The engine was a little noisy, but it seemed to run smoothly. He'd had seat belts installed, and the leather seats must have been reupholstered at least once.

The traffic in Ghirardelli Square was light, and soon Jared pulled into a multilevel parking lot. "I always take forever to find just the right parking place, so I hope you can bear with me," he told her. "I try to make sure no one will bump my car. The plastic-and-fiberglass creations people drive today would be destroyed in a skirmish with this hulk."

Rebecca scowled playfully. "Don't tell me you're actually one of those horrible people who take up two parking spaces so no one can scratch their cars?"

Jared pulled neatly into a corner slot between the wall and a pillar. "I've never been guilty of that particular sin."

She looked at him in the harsh fluorescent light. He was wearing a beautiful gray suit with a pale green tint. With his hair shorter he looked younger, a little more vulnerable. His eyebrows were almost bushy, shielding deep-set dark eyes. Although she'd never cared much for mustaches, she found herself thinking his neatly trimmed mustache wasn't too bad, actually. It seemed a completely natural addition to his handsome, very masculine face.

She put her fingers on the door handle and he shook his head. "I'll get the door for you."

First flowers, now he insisted on opening the door for her. She hadn't expected old-fashioned gallantry from him. Being treated like a frail maiden made her feel a little silly, especially since she had never been small and dainty, but it also made her feel special. She stepped out easily when he opened the door, and they walked to the square, where they took the elevator up to the restaurant.

They sat down side by side on a soft, pale pink banquette to wait for their table. Having refused a drink, Rebecca looked around the restaurant with interest. The decor was similar to what she had seen in movies of colonial India, rather heavy furniture upholstered in slightly garish pastels with a lot of greenery around. Huge glass windows provided a view of the bay and the night sky, and she was delighted when she and Jared were taken upstairs to a table right next to a window. Jared and the headwaiter solicitously seated her in the position with the best view, and again she had the unusual sensation of being pampered. She opened the large menu and studied the descriptions of unfamiliar dishes.

Jared watched her as she pored over the menu. Her face was glowing, her eyes bright; she seemed as pleased as a child at a birthday party. Of course she'd been taken out to dinner a thousand times before, he told himself. Could it be that she liked him? Maybe the color in her cheeks was due to the drink she'd had at her place. Whatever the cause, she seemed to be having a good time, and the thought warmed him. She was so lovely in the rosy light of the restaurant, her features soft despite her severe hairstyle.

He glanced at the menu. "If you like very spicy

foods, we could have the chicken chat as an appetizer."

She looked up at him. "I know all about chicken chat. Cluck cluck cluck."

Despite himself, he laughed. "That's the worst pun I've ever heard."

She smiled, a small Mona Lisa curve of her lips that he hadn't seen before, and he leaned toward her as she said, "Today's the first day I've ever made a pun, so have patience. Maybe I'll get better with practice."

"Maybe you will." Her hand was resting on the table, and he reached across to cover it with his own, stroking the curve of her thumb with the ball of his own. Her skin was wonderfully soft and smooth. He should have taken the chair next to hers instead of sitting across the table. He wanted to be near her, to be able to lean very close when she spoke, close enough to smell her perfume, almost close enough to kiss her.

Her eyes were darkening; then she lowered her lids suddenly and they were no longer looking at each other. Her cheeks had a faint tint of pink, but her features were immobile. For a moment, before she had looked down, he had been sure their physical attraction was mutual. Now, caressing her hand with the tips of his fingers, he wasn't so sure. He wanted her, there was no question about that, but it was probably too soon to wonder if she felt the same way about him. They hardly knew each other, after all. But that could be remedied.

"Have you ever been married?" he asked, and she looked up quickly, freezing like a startled rabbit.

What kind of question was that? she wondered, gently pulling her hand away and putting it in her lap. She couldn't keep up with him. One minute they were reading the menu and joking, and the next minute he was holding her hand and asking for her life story. The touch of his hand had been very pleasant, she didn't deny that. It had made her feel very feminine and desirable, and the soft stroking of his fingers had irresistibly awakened thoughts of touching him more intimately. So why was she resisting his advance, if that was what it was. It wasn't as if she had an extensive history of marriages and love affairs too lurid to recount. Or maybe that *was* the problem. She wished she had more of a past and could be more his equal in experience. She was at a disadvantage, knowing so little about men, unsure if he was really attracted to her or if his behavior was natural gallantry.

"No, I've never been married," she answered. He was probably divorced himself. Maybe even more than once.

"Engaged?"

She shook her head. "So far I've paid more attention to my career than to anything else. Somehow I never found much time for love and romance—or maybe love and romance never found time for me."

He seemed to be scrutinizing her, as if he didn't believe what she was saying. "But there have been men in your life?"

She looked out the window at the dark waters of the bay. Teenage romances were not what he meant. "Just a few," she answered. *After all, one was a few. A very few.* "What about you?"

"I was engaged once, briefly. Aside from that, I've never had the remotest desire to marry. In fact, I don't think I wanted to get married even then. It was just a momentary weakness. I realized quickly enough that marriage wasn't for me, and Joan and I are still friends."

They gave their orders to the waiter, then Rebecca

began playing with her fork. "What do you have against marriage?"

His face was very serious, and he touched his mustache in a gesture that was becoming familiar. "I can see in my family and in my friends that people weren't made to pair off together for a lifetime. In three or four years people grow tired of each other. They stop loving each other, and they can either divorce or slog on together in bored misery. I don't like either alternative."

"Did your parents get divorced?" The waiter appeared with their wine, and she waited while Jared tasted it and the waiter poured.

"No, my father died when I was twelve. My mother's had three husbands since then."

"Well," Rebecca began, "maybe she was trying to replace your father and never found anyone else she loved as much."

He laughed, a soft, bitter laugh that chilled her. "She'd like you to think that, I'm sure. That she lost the one true love of her life. You must be quite a romantic."

She shook her head emphatically. "I've always thought of myself as a realist, and I'm sure not all marriages are unhappy. Some people are made to be married, and some aren't. It's just a matter of figuring out which group you're in."

He was silent while their steaming plates were arranged on the table. The spicy aroma of her lamb curry piqued her appetite, and she waited a little impatiently for all the dishes to be arranged on the table.

"And which group are you in?" Jared asked when the waiter left.

It took her a few seconds to understand his question. "Oh, I doubt if I'll ever marry. It doesn't have much appeal for me, to be honest."

He raised his wineglass with a crooked smile. "To solitary bliss," he said, and for some reason she was a little reluctant to join in the toast.

"There's a lot of middle ground between marriage and solitude," she told him, and his smile broadened.

"To the middle ground, then," he said, and she lifted her glass, wondering if she'd said more than she intended to.

Her curry was not quite as spicy as the menu had threatened, and she ate it happily, enjoying the tingling sensation in her mouth and lips. Jared appeared to be equally pleased with his lamb dish, and they devoted themselves to their meals for a few minutes.

"Since we're both having lamb, shouldn't you tell a few sheep jokes?" she asked.

"Well, one does come to mind, but I promised myself I wouldn't make any puns tonight. After all, I have a serious side too."

She thought for a moment, taking a sip of wine. "Maybe you can make the pun into a riddle."

"Of course. Well, then, what do you use when you take your female sheep to market?"

Rebecca's eyes narrowed, then inspiration made her sit up very straight. "A ewe-haul trailer!" she said, laughing.

He looked at her with a faint smile, an expression on his face that she couldn't interpret. His dark gaze remained on her and made her feel a little self-conscious. She knew that to glance away would be an act of cowardice, but she could hardly eat with him looking at her like that. He reached across the table for her hand.

Rebecca began to suspect that things were moving a little too fast for her. She'd never dated a man she wasn't already acquainted with, so she had nothing to compare this evening to. She'd only spent a few hours with Jared Wells, and here he was playing with her fingers, caressing them until every nerve ending came alive. She knew her face was flushed at this point, as much from nervousness as from the erotic sensations his touch was provoking in her.

"How is your sister coming along?" she asked him, nonchalantly sliding her hand away from his and picking up her fork.

His smile broadened for an instant, as if he knew her motives for redirecting the conversation. Then he grew serious. "She's started gaining a few pounds every week, which I guess is typical of someone who hasn't had the problem very long. And Dr. Fairweather actually talked Sybil and George into attending two family information meetings. So I have the impression things are going pretty well."

"Good." She took another sip of wine. "I told you that I think very highly of Alice."

"The feeling seems to be mutual. It's funny, but I discovered that I already knew her. She owns a cabin near our family vacation place in San Luis Obispo County, and for years I've been seeing her around the lake and at the general store, but we never introduced ourselves. I've always thought she was rather attractive."

He looked quite pleased with himself, and she suppressed a twinge of jealousy by telling herself that Alice couldn't date him and treat his sister at the same time. The waiter cleared the table and returned with the dessert tray, and Rebecca examined a rather mysterious white square topped with something gold and shiny.

"That gold will wreak havoc with your teeth," Jared warned her. "If I were you, I'd pick something else."

"Is this real gold?" Rebecca asked, and the waiter nodded.

"The thin layer of gold on top makes this a very special dessert for honored guests," he explained.

Rebecca lifted her eyebrows. "In that case, how can I refuse?" she said, and selected one small square.

"Are you always so adventurous?" Jared asked as she took her first bite of the foil.

"If you consider eating a new dessert an adventure," Rebecca answered, wincing a little at the sensation of the gold against a metal filling. "I've never traveled to exotic lands the way you have." She finished the square quickly.

"I assume from the expression on your face that it wasn't your favorite dessert. Would you like to go somewhere else for coffee and something sweet?" Jared asked, and she shook her head.

"We can have coffee at my place, if you don't mind instant." At his look she added, "And I have tea."

"Tea sounds good," he said dryly.

They walked downstairs, retrieved her jacket, and were quickly in the car. She watched him out of the corner of her eye as he drove. Maybe she had made a mistake in inviting him in. Since they had left the restaurant, he hadn't touched her again, but of course that told her nothing about what might happen later. She found him very attractive, but she hoped he wouldn't expect much more than a drink from her this evening.

Aside from everything else, she wasn't ready for him to realize how inexperienced she was, and he'd probably know that from her nervousness if they kissed. Whatever her mother had told her long ago, Rebecca knew that it was hardly fashionable to have reached the advanced age of twenty-nine being single and having had only one lover. It was true that she'd been very busy, first studying and working to pay for her education and then just working. But if she'd been more gregarious, more sexy, more something, there would have been more men in her life. And once he knew the truth, she feared Jared would start to wonder what was wrong with her.

She passed him her card to open the gate, and he drove to her condominium. Still in the car, he turned toward her and she looked away involuntarily, her nerves tingling.

"Does the invitation still stand?" he asked softly, and she turned back to face him.

"Of course."

"You've seemed a little subdued since we left the restaurant. Are you tired?"

She shook her head, and moved to open the door.

"I do that, remember?" He leaned across to touch her hand and she let go of the door handle, waiting for him to walk around the car and open the door. He hesitated a moment, looking at her, and she felt a nervous quiver deep within her. Then he was out of the car, her door was open, and she stepped out onto the sidewalk, ignoring his outstretched hand. It was true that she was a little nervous, but she could still manage the everyday tasks of life without his assistance. She unlocked her door and led him inside, grateful that the lighted rooms seemed safe and ordinary enough to banish her attack of nerves.

"Herb tea or regular?" she asked, and he shrugged.

"Regular, I guess. Do you really have only instant coffee?"

"It's all I drink." She put the teakettle on the stove, then selected two mugs and set them out on the counter.

He moved closer to her, and she turned away to get the tea. As she took the first step, his hand brushed her arm lightly. When she looked into his eyes her heart began to pound faster. There was no mistaking his seductive intent.

"So tell me about Nepal," she said. He shook his head once. "Another time."

She knew beyond any doubt that he would kiss her unless she moved away. She could step back, just a few steps, and that would be the end of it. But he'd never understand. He'd assume she didn't find him attractive, and she'd never see him again. She was too nervous to feel anything but anxiety as she watched him lean toward her.

He wasn't holding her, wasn't touching her at all. They stood there like soldiers on parade, hands at their sides, and his lips brushed tentatively against hers. His mustache tickled her upper lip very faintly, and the sensation surprised her for an instant until she realized what it was. His lips were warm and dry, and she hardly had time to wonder how she should respond before it was over.

"Okay?" he asked very quietly, and she nodded.

Then his lips were there again, pressing gently against hers, his mustache prickling softly against her skin. He was being so gentle, his kiss was so tender, that she began to feel less hesitant. It was a very undemanding kiss, more a way of getting acquainted than a passionate demand.

His lips moved against hers, a little more insistently this time, encouraging her to kiss him back. When she sighed with pleasure, his hands moved to stroke her arms and shoulders through her silk dress, a calm, soothing touch that made her lean a little closer to him. Then, for the first time, their bodies touched, swaying warmly together, and she luxuriated in the sensation of being wrapped in his arms, pressed against his hard, warm chest.

Gradually, as his tender kisses chased away her self-consciousness and inhibitions, her mind stopped whirling, stopped wondering whether he was disappointed in her, and she ran her hands up his back under his jacket, her fingers caressing the muscles there. She rubbed his back, enjoying the warmth she could feel through the fabric of his shirt, and then pulled away briefly to free her hands and put her arms over his shoulders. His newly cut hair was a little bristly on the back of his neck, she discovered as she resumed the kiss.

When she leaned against him more fully so that their lower bodies were touching, she was immediately aware of his arousal. The solid maleness of him seemed to call forth a response from her body, and without realizing it she crossed the line between a gentle, exploratory kiss and a passionate embrace. Her hands caressed the back of his neck urgently as her body pressed tightly against his. He wrapped his arms around her shoulders, as if to pull her even closer, but she could sense that he wasn't as fully infected with her growing excitement as she wanted him to be. Delicately she probed his mouth with her tongue, and he made a low sound deep in his throat. One of his hands moved to her buttocks, and she felt a thrill of satisfaction as his caresses grew more demanding. She never would have thought it possible, but she was quite willing to go to bed with him that very night. In fact, she was prepared to insist on it.

CHAPTER FOUR

He had meant it to be no more than a warm, soft, get-acquainted kind of kiss, something that would confirm to each of them that the chemistry was there if they wanted to pursue the relationship. The sudden fierce hunger of her response, her tongue caressing his, almost cost him his control. It had been a long time since he'd kissed anyone, and he had been afraid of putting her off with a sudden onslaught of passion, but obviously he couldn't predict her responses as well as he had thought.

The soft swell of her breasts against his chest, the pressure of her slender thighs against his, the warm movements of her lips, were enough to dissolve his earlier resolutions. What better way to learn to know each other than by the slow exploration of each other's bodies, by tenderly discovering and meeting each other's deepest needs? He knew with absolute certainty that an incomparable night lay ahead, and suddenly it was easy once again to keep his urgency within bounds. They had all the time in the world.

As naturally as if he'd known her for months, he slid one hand along the slippery silk of her dress until his palm encountered an erect nipple, delightfully obvious even through several layers of cloth. He caressed her lovingly, enjoying her faint sighs of pleasure, vaguely aware of a sibilant noise to one side of him.

With his other hand he continued to stroke her buttocks, reveling in the firm, round flesh he could feel beneath the dress. The warmth of their bodies released the scent of her perfume, which seemed now to have a lemony tang that aroused his nostrils.

He moved his hand to her hair, sliding his fingers under the smooth, thick wave at the side of her head, gently pulling it loose from the gold clasp so that he could almost run his fingers through it. Her hair was finer than he had expected, very soft to touch, and faintly fragrant of shampoo. He was tempted to take the clasp off, to bury both his hands in her hair, but somehow the gesture seemed to take too much for granted.

He kissed her cheek softly, then moved his lips gently along the line of her jaw to the spot just under her ear. It was nice that she was tall, he mused as he returned to savor her lips. He could kiss her without stooping or crouching, and their bodies fitted well together.

She pressed a little closer to him, and his thoughts were less coherent as he ran his hands lightly down her body, loving the length of her, the firmness of her muscles. He would willingly have stood there for hours, learning the contours of her body, finding out what touches gave her the most pleasure, but their position was a little awkward, and the kitchen was hardly the ideal spot for extended lovemaking.

"Let's go into the other room," he suggested huskily a second before a piercing whistle startled them both. It was the teakettle, and quickly he reached behind Rebecca to turn off the burner. But he wasn't turning the right knob, because the uncomfortably high-pitched whistle became even more shrill. Feeling Rebecca pulling away from him, he moved his hand hurriedly and made searing contact with the glowing electric coil.

"Damn!" he exclaimed as he jerked away. The shrieking whistle died down to a faint whimper as she moved the kettle, and they looked at each other.

"Is your hand all right?" she asked, concerned. "Let me get you some ice."

Her eyes seemed a little out of focus, dazed by their recent passion, and her lips looked voluptuously swollen from the lengthy kisses they'd shared only moments ago. She swayed a little as she moved toward the refrigerator, and he felt a mysterious and powerful emotion at the sight of her confusion. They had been wrenched out of a timeless moment, too suddenly hit with the realization that they were two people who were getting to know each other, hardly ready yet to become lovers.

Rebecca emptied an ice tray and wrapped a couple of cubes in a clean dishcloth.

"Let me see your hand," she said as she moved toward Jared, uncomfortably aware of her nipples and the swollen heat between her thighs.

"It's nothing, really. More an irritation than anything," he said, taking the ice from her and pressing it against the red streak on the side of his hand.

Just standing near the man made hot sensations stir within her. "I'll make the tea," she said quickly, "since that's why we came in here in the first place." For some reason she couldn't find the yellow packets of Earl Grey tea. *Calm down,* she ordered herself.

She wasn't surprised that she was so strongly attracted to Jared, but the intensity of her response to him had startled and almost frightened her. Looking back, she knew that never once had she wanted Ed so desperately, so overwhelmingly. And she had loved Ed, trusted and depended on him. But over the months of their relationship, his practiced lovemaking had never aroused her the way Jared's kisses had.

"Is this what you're looking for?" Jared's arm appeared over her shoulder, his hand dangling the tea bags in front of her. "We'll need some cups," he added, and she shook her head.

"I'm on a distant planet tonight, I guess."

"Wherever you are, I'd like to be there with you."

His eyes searched her face and she looked away, putting two sage-colored mugs on the counter for him to drop the tea bags into. She wasn't ready to respond to his hinted desire for more closeness—not until she had thought things through. She poured the steaming water into the mugs, leaning over them to enjoy the sweet bergamot scent of the tea.

"If only this tasted as good as it smells," she remarked, leading him out to the living room, "it would be worth a fortune."

She sat down on the sofa, feeling a little startled when he sat right next to her. There was a scant inch of space between them, and right now she needed to feel a little farther from him than that.

"Let me just say that I don't want to take things any further than you're comfortable with." His voice was gentle, and she looked directly into his eyes, certain now that he was telling her the unvarnished truth. All she had to do was tell him how she felt. Not that she understood everything she was feeling, but she did know that things had moved much too quickly tonight.

"I lost my head for a moment," she said. "I'd like us to have time to get better acquainted." She watched him, hoping for a sign that he understood and agreed.

His eyes crinkled mischievously. "I thought that's what we were doing earlier."

"Getting better acquainted?" She raised her eyebrows.

"I've heard it said that sex is an excellent way of getting to know people," he said, taking a sip of tea.

"It'll never replace tea and cookies after church," Rebecca replied playfully.

"And I thought it already had," Jared said, shaking his head and balancing his mug on his knee.

Rebecca laughed. "I admit I haven't been to church much lately, but I doubt that the social events have changed that much since I was young." She relaxed back into the sofa cushions.

"I suppose not." He smiled a little, but his gaze was watchful.

His thigh was at least three inches from hers now, but she was certain she could still feel the heat from his skin on her own leg. It was difficult to think, to keep the conversation going. The scent of bergamot rose softly from their mugs, and she stifled a sigh.

Her eyes were drawn to his mustache, which had felt so much softer than it looked. She remembered its tickling caress against her lip and wondered how it would feel in the hollow of her shoulder, or against her breast. Sometime she would like to touch it with her finger, smooth it down and then brush it upward, to feel both its softness and bristliness.

"You've fallen quiet again," he said, smiling as if he knew the direction of her thoughts, and she nodded.

"I was thinking what a nice evening it's been."

He grinned and stood up, holding out his hands to her, and she realized that they'd finished drinking their tea. "It has been nice, and I suppose that was a subtle hint that it's over now. I know we both have to go to work tomorrow."

She laid her hands in his and allowed him to draw

her to her feet and toward his chest. If he kissed her again, she wasn't sure she'd be able to send him away.

He pulled her gently against him, her breasts pressing softly into his chest, and with complete astonishment she felt his lips brush her forehead. Surely that wouldn't be the end of it. She stayed there, leaning against his chest, and felt her body's immediate reaction to his nearness. His response was similar; she could feel it. And again she was unwilling to interrupt what seemed to be inevitable. It was as if they were on a planet with twice the earth's gravity. She felt heavy, feverish, overwhelmingly lethargic. It was impossible to move away from him.

She could smell a faint scent of soap or shaving lotion on his cheek, a slightly spicy smell, and she nuzzled the warm skin under his ear. She kissed his neck and then his cheek, moving toward his lips. Her breasts seemed to swell against him in anticipation. She remembered the sensation of his fingers on her nipples, his hands stroking her buttocks, and she sucked a long breath into her lungs.

"If I'm going to leave tonight," he began, and she forced herself to pay attention, "I'd better do it now."

"I suppose," she said breathily, wanting to keep him there, wanting to run her hands all over him. She'd better take some time to think things over, she knew, even though her body seemed to sigh a protest as she and Jared separated. She brought her hands to her sides, releasing him as he pulled away.

"You haven't told me a thing about Nepal," she called after him when he carried his cup into the kitchen. "And I was really looking forward to hearing about your stay there."

He stood at the front door, his hand on the doorknob. "I imagine that if I promised to show you all my slides on our next date, this would turn out to be our last date."

She grinned. "How many slides do you have?"

"Thousands." He was looking a little sheepish, and she enjoyed that. It made him seem more vulnerable, a little less smooth than he had seemed earlier.

"I think I could sit through a few hundred carefully selected slides," she said, and he nodded.

"That's settled, then. I'll call you in a few days to set up a time. Maybe I'll barbecue some chicken. But once the slide show starts, the doors and windows lock automatically and you're not permitted to leave for any reason."

Rebecca wrinkled her nose. "Now that I think of it, I'm going to be awfully busy for the next several weeks. I'm not sure I have time for more than a few photographs."

He reached out and touched her arm very softly. "I have photographs too. Albums and albums of them."

His hand was warm, and the touch of his fingers seemed to linger on her skin after he'd taken his hand away. She wanted to press her palm over her arm, to keep the sensation a few seconds longer. Her body yearned for him. Even the slightest caress would soothe her, she thought, although she would prefer to be pressed tightly against his chest, to have his arms curve around her, to feel his excitement crescendo again.

"To be honest, I'd probably love to see every slide and photograph you have. But maybe not all at once."

"That's understandable." Again he reached for her, but only to grip her arms. She rested her hands lightly on the rough fabric of his jacket, not absolutely sure that she wanted him to stay, but unable to let him go. They couldn't stand at the door indefinitely, and she wasn't quite confident enough to pull him back to the sofa or over to the stairs. As he had said earlier, tomorrow was a workday, and anyway, she reminded herself, she needed time.

"So we'll get together sometime next weekend?" he said, and she smiled. That was much nicer than the usual vague promise of a phone call. Maybe now she could actually bring herself to say good night.

She leaned toward him and brushed her lips against his. She wasn't about to settle for a kiss on the forehead this time, not after the erotic intensity they'd shared earlier in the evening. Anything less than a fully arousing kiss would negate what had gone before, and she wanted him to remember how good things could be between them. She ran her hands up the back of his jacket, smoothing the cloth over his shoulderblades, pressing her thumbs into the muscles that ridged his spine.

Deliberately she flicked her tongue between his lips, marveling at his stillness. Her own excitement was building, fueled by her efforts to arouse him more. She wanted him to lie awake tonight thinking of her the way she knew she'd be thinking of him. She grew a little more daring with her tongue, caressing the inside of his mouth. Then she heard the sharp exhalation of his breath before his hands moved to her shoulders and pulled her forward fiercely. His lips ground into hers almost painfully, and his hands moved quickly down her back to press her firmly against his pelvis. Even more strongly she felt the urgent need of her body to know him, to be touched by him, to feel his skin against hers. She moved her fingers across his chest, wondering how it would feel if he were naked. She tried to imagine what his bare chest looked like, if his nipples would be very sensitive to her tongue.

"This time," he said with a groan, his breath warm in her ear, "I really will leave. And to preserve your good reputation in the neighborhood, I suggest you turn the porch light off before I go."

"What . . ." she began, then glanced involuntarily at his tailored slacks as she realized what he was talking about.

"I just don't want to call undue attention to my condition," he explained dryly.

She glanced down again and stifled a laugh. The kiss had certainly had the desired effect. Jared opened the door, and she folded her arms against the chilly draft of air.

"Good night," he said with a gentle smile, and suddenly he was gone.

Feeling slightly dizzy but happy, she went into the kitchen and put the two mugs in the dishwasher. How had they survived the hours they'd spent together without making love? It had seemed the obvious next step at least twice, yet somehow they had resisted the temptation. Or at least Jared had. At certain moments this evening she would have gone to bed with him willingly, even eagerly. She'd been saved once by the teakettle, but after that it had been Jared who had prevented their physical attraction from running away with them. Looking back on it, the evening seemed to have been one long embrace, a prelude to intimacy that never occurred. Surely on their next evening they would take the big step.

Turning off the lights on her way, she climbed the stairs to her bedroom, and within a few minutes she was pulling the rainbow quilt up under her chin. It was too easy to imagine Jared in bed with her. It would have been exactly right to turn to him, to lay her cheek against the hollow of his shoulder. She rolled over on her stomach. She would put herself to sleep imagining that she was walking through a meadow, a technique that never failed. Tomorrow would be soon enough to think about Jared Wells.

The next morning she managed to lose her keys twice before she left the house and was barely in time for her first appointment. She'd had a restless night. Her sleep had been filled with dreams of unidentified men, men with knowing hands and urgent mouths. She'd even dreamed of Ed, for the first time in two months, experiencing again in her sleep the chest-aching pain of their good-bye. None of this was good, as far as Rebecca was concerned. In order to do her best work, she needed to be clear-headed and able to concentrate on what her patients were saying and doing, and she would have to make sure she regained that state of mind very quickly.

All day she felt distracted, finding that between patients, when she should have been making notes, she was lapsing into daydreams. She imagined herself in Jared's arms, lying naked against his skin, and her body ached for him. His caresses, his kisses, seemed to haunt her free moments, and she was thankful to be able to banish thoughts of him when patients were in her office.

By four o'clock that afternoon she felt more in command of herself, which was encouraging, since she was seeing a court-referred family. These were usually her most difficult cases, since often none of the family members wanted therapy. They tended to be silent and uncooperative and, to make matters worse, they rarely paid their bills. Rebecca felt it was her obligation to have three or four such families in her caseload, on the chance that she might be of help to them.

This particular family had been referred because the twelve-year-old son had been found driving the family car without a license. According to the information the boy's mother had given her over the phone, this was a family with three teenagers, so Rebecca was braced for a large, sullen group. Instead, only the father appeared, red-faced and nervous.

"I had to leave work fifteen minutes early," he began. "And my sons have softball practice tonight, so they won't be able to make it."

Rebecca took her appointment book from the desk drawer. "Perhaps we can find a better time for your appointment, then."

"There's really no reason to do that," he said, reaching into his jacket pocket. "My son was just behaving like a normal red-blooded boy. His older brothers drive, so of course he wants to also. He's a good kid."

"I'm sure he is," Rebecca agreed. "But according to the information his probation officer sent me, this is the sixth time he's been found driving your car. That must be a problem for you and your family."

"Well, we do have to go down and get him from the police station, that sort of thing. But it's nothing compared to the problems a weekly appointment with you will cause."

"This is court-ordered therapy," Rebecca said. "I'm sure you were given a choice of several psychologists, but you will have to spend the time somewhere. If you miss an appointment, I'm required to report it to your son's probation officer."

"Exactly. So I'll pay you for six months in advance. Just so you know we'll be here every week." He gave her an exaggerated wink, and she suddenly realized what he was suggesting: that she accept payment in return for lying to the probation officer.

"If you and the other four members of your family don't appear like clockwork every week, I'll be on the phone to your son's probation officer by the end of the hour." She was angry, and it showed. She could feel the acceleration of her heartbeat, her quickened breathing, and she tried to calm down.

"You can be as high and mighty as you want," he said, standing and opening the door. "I'll just find someone else who's willing to play it my way. Thanks for nothing."

The door slammed behind him, and Rebecca rested her forehead on her palm. She'd handled the situation exactly wrong. As he'd said, she'd gotten high and mighty and paid more attention to her own outrage than to his desire to avoid therapy. If she'd listened to him more carefully, been more sympathetic to his understandable desire to believe that his son had no problems, maybe she could have accomplished something. As it was, she'd only made things harder for the next psychologist and reinforced the father's hostility.

She ran her hand lightly over the surface of the desk, wishing her old friend Marian were still alive. She needed someone to talk to about her occasional failures, needed to express her own disappointment in herself, and there wasn't anyone available for that. As a student, she'd always had a supervisor, and in the clinic there'd been plenty of willing ears. But this sense of isolation was the price she paid for independence. Maybe she'd try talking to Cal later, she decided.

She saw two more families and made it through the sessions somehow, but she was feeling guilty and still worrying about her earlier lapse of judgment. Not since her student days had she felt so inadequate as a therapist. She was letting one incident bother her too much, she knew, and she hoped a good night's sleep would straighten things out in her mind and relieve some of the pressure she was feeling.

Once she had arrived home and fed Ferdinand and Isabella, she went immediately to the refrigerator and peered disconsolately inside. Late Sunday afternoon was the time for her usual grocery store visit, and somehow yesterday, because of her dinner date with Jared, she'd forgotten that all her cupboards were bare. It was eight o'clock, she was starving, and in fact the whole day had been a disaster.

She was a little tempted to blame everything on Jared. If it hadn't been for him, she'd have a refrigerator full of food, she'd have done a much better job with her patients, and her life would be as calm and orderly as usual. Of course it wasn't really Jared who was disrupting things; it was her attraction to him, the way she couldn't get him out of her mind. Her emotions were coloring everything, distracting her from more important concerns, making her overly sensitive and thin-skinned.

As she contemplated a small bowl of dried-up tuna salad, the phone rang. It was Madeleine with an offer of leftover spaghetti, and Rebecca thankfully ground up the tuna in the garbage disposal and tried to think of a contribution she could make to the dinner. There was a pint of ice cream in the freezer—certainly a better choice than the lone can of pickled beets in the cupboard—so she grabbed it and left.

"Cal just called and said he was eating out," Madeleine said when she opened the door. "I hope you don't mind filling in for him at the last minute."

Rebecca put the ice cream in Madeleine's freezer and sat down at the kitchen table, which was already set for two.

"I suppose I'm a poor substitute for Cal," she said, "but I'm very glad to be here. My kitchen is even less well stocked than usual, and I was too tired and too hungry to go shopping."

Madeleine nodded as she filled the plates. "The truth is . . ." She hesitated, and Rebecca noticed a pink tinge creeping up her cheeks. "I'm embarrassed to admit it, but I just accidentally noticed last night that you had a date." She sat down, her pale eyes wide. "I recognized him as the man from Nepal, and I've been dying to find out if you had a good time. But I didn't want you to feel as if you don't have any privacy."

Rebecca wolfed down several bites of spaghetti, unperturbed, as Madeleine twisted her spaghetti on the fork on her plate. "I just happened to be standing at the window," she went on, and Rebecca laughed.

"I don't mind at all, so stop worrying. And yes, I had a very good time." The tangy oregano smell of the spaghetti sauce had increased her appetite to ravenous, but now that her plate was half empty she was beginning to feel content. "I'm afraid I've made a pig out of myself," she said.

"Tell me more about last night," Madeleine said, "and I'll give you what's left in the pot. Otherwise I'll take it all myself. Would you like to see him again?"

Rebecca chased a stray strand of spaghetti around her plate with her fork. "Yes and no," she said finally. "I'm afraid of having my professional life and my personal life all disorganized and disrupted again. It's not fair to my patients, and it's not good for me."

Madeleine smiled her Mona Lisa smile. "So he's someone who can disrupt your life, is he? Then I'd say he's as good for you as anyone could be." She seemed to be lost in her own private thoughts for a few seconds, and they were obviously happy ones. "You need someone to love, someone who can take your breath away and make you forget your patients for a while."

"Then I wouldn't be as good a therapist as I am," Rebecca replied.

After Rebecca declined Madeleine's offer of more spaghetti, Madeleine stood to clear the table, pressing her hands into the small of her back in what had become a familiar gesture. "Maybe not so good in some ways, but I'll bet you'd be better in other ways. Doesn't every human experience deepen your understanding of other people?"

Rebecca rubbed her forehead. Madeleine was suggesting, in the nicest possible way, that a single, nearly virginal woman could hardly hope to understand fully the problems of married couples and their children. And maybe her solitary life did mean that she was abnormal and in no position to offer therapy to others. Still, she had helped people; she knew she had. And she owed her success to her dedication, her willingness to concentrate fully on her patients.

Madeleine sat down again, her face very serious as she pushed her blond hair back from her ears. "Maybe I shouldn't tell you this, but Cal thinks you've been trying to model yourself on Marian Blanchard, dedicating yourself exclusively to your patients the way she did instead of getting married and having a family too."

Rebecca shook her head. "Maybe he's right." She was relieved to hear Cal open the front door, knowing that once he joined them, Madeleine would drop the subject. In fact, Cal immediately began talking about a new staff member at the clinic, and to Rebecca's quiet satisfaction, the topic of her personal life never arose.

When conversation lagged she brought up her experience with the court-referred family, and Cal was amused by her dismay. "You're well rid of that case, I'd say. Once I leave the clinic, I'll never touch an involuntary patient. So stop criticizing yourself and count your blessings instead."

Rebecca wrinkled her nose. "I'll try." It was late; time for her to wash the dishes and go. Somehow she couldn't do as Cal suggested and be glad she'd scared

72

the man off. She'd had patients leave before—many times, in fact—but in those cases she'd always known that she'd done her best. Today she'd been almost at her worst.

She thanked Cal and Madeleine and walked home. It was early still, but she decided to curl up in bed with a few journals and see if she couldn't somehow return to her old self. She had a heavy day tomorrow, and she intended to do a terrific job all day long.

As it turned out, she didn't do a terrific job, but she was reasonably satisfied with her day. After work she went grocery shopping and had a late dinner at home, half expecting that Jared would call about the weekend. He didn't call that night or the next, and despite real qualms about seeing him again, she was dismayed at the thought that he might not call at all. It had never occurred to her until then that he might have been insincere, that he might have had no intention of following through. Surely her judgment of people was better than that.

He finally called late Thursday night, and her heart thudded erratically as she recognized his voice. "I hope you don't mind my calling so late in the week," he said. "I've been quite busy, and each time I decided to call, it seemed to be too late at night. I didn't want to wake you."

"I still have plenty of free time this weekend," she said lightly, "so don't worry." Her earlier fears about being involved with him seemed to have vanished. She felt happier than she had in weeks—months even.

"Speaking of worrying," Jared said, "I wonder if you could give me some friendly advice about my sister."

She leaned against the kitchen wall, twisting the telephone cord in her fingers. "I don't want to intrude

73

on Alice's territory," she said, reluctant to refuse him such a simple thing, "but what's the problem?"

"Well, to put it bluntly, Meri's become quite obnoxious. She slams around the house refusing to do anything she's asked, she doesn't come home from school on time, and I guess Sybil and George are ready to pull her out of therapy."

Rebecca straightened. "Don't let them do it! It sounds to me as if your sister is doing just fine.

"It's a common mistake to stop therapy when a child's behavior changes, because it's unsettling for the parents to have new problems to handle. But change is what therapy is all about. As long as your sister's gaining weight, I'd assume everything's going according to plan."

"That's what I wanted to know." His voice was a little deeper now, more relaxed, and she warmed to the sound of it. "I'll keep the pressure on them to continue seeing Dr. Fairweather. Maybe I'll drop by there tomorrow after dinner and see how things are going."

There was a brief silence, then he said, "I shouldn't have given this second place in the conversation, really. Now you'll think I only want you for your free consulting."

She laughed, but a little hesitantly. His sister had brought them together, and Rebecca didn't really object to the idea that Meredith's problems might give Jared extra incentive to call her. That was okay as long as Meredith wasn't the only reason he wanted to see her. Remembering his heart pounding against her chest, she didn't really imagine that Jared's interest in her was strictly professional.

"Would you like to have dinner at my place Saturday?" Jared was saying. "I'm quite a good cook, and then there are the famous slides and photographs for after-dinner entertainment."

"I imagine we'll find plenty to entertain us after dinner," Rebecca said huskily, surprising herself a little, and basked in the warm laugh that caressed her ear.

"So you'll come?" he asked.

"Of course. I'll be looking forward to it." She didn't really want to end the conversation, but it would have been awkward not to, once she had his address and telephone number.

After their good-byes, she hung up the phone very gently and bent to stroke Ferdinand's back. Her present happiness couldn't last forever—that wasn't the way life worked—but she could certainly enjoy it for the next few hours. She felt like imitating one of those ridiculous old movie scenes, dancing around the kitchen with the phone clutched to her breast. Impulsively she scooped Ferdinand up off the floor, but he gave an indignant yowl and twisted out of her arms.

"So much for your movie career," she called to him as his stiffly affronted tail disappeared around the door.

CHAPTER FIVE

Saturday morning Rebecca was awakened by the sun illuminating the pale yellow shutters of her bedroom. She sat up with a start, thinking that if the fog had already burned off, she must have overslept. In fact the clock showed that it was only seven-thirty, and she opened the shutters exuberantly. The sky was clear, the leaves on the trees were shiny, and everything pointed to an unusually warm day in the city. And if it was warm in the city, it would be very hot on the peninsula. Of course, for a resident of San Francisco, an occasional heat wave was something to relish. It was good to have the opportunity to bake out the damp fog, to soak up the heat that would help her survive the damp, cold days ahead.

The kitchen, usually coolly austere in the morning, was sparkling with sunshine, and when Rebecca opened the front door a crack the temperature seemed to be already in the high sixties. Holding her cotton robe tightly at the neck, she leaned out quickly to pick up her newspaper. This morning she would scramble eggs, she decided, in celebration of the weather. As she had told Jared, she almost never cooked, so making two eggs was for her as big a gesture as eggs Benedict might be for a more accomplished cook. Not wanting to risk failure, she scrambled them in the microwave with a little oregano, studying the cookbook directions carefully as she proceeded. The water had boiled for her instant coffee by the time she gave the eggs their last stir, and she sat down happily to her breakfast, spreading out the rather skimpy Saturday paper over her oak kitchen table. Soon, however, her mind began wandering.

She was looking forward to tonight's dinner with Jared. Well, not exactly the dinner, although barbecued chicken was fine. But she enjoyed being with Jared, and the sexual tingle of anticipation she felt when she thought about seeing him was quite pleasant. Then a sobering thought struck her. Was it possible that their early meetings had been weighted by fantasy, so that tonight she would be disappointed in him? And then recalling what had gone on in this very room last Sunday, she doubted that very much.

After washing her breakfast dishes she went upstairs to shower and dress. She had a few patients this morning. After seeing them, maybe she'd go for a swim at the club she belonged to near her office. She could sit in the sun until late afternoon and catch up on her journals, then drive back home in time to get ready for the evening.

She returned to the city late in the afternoon, pleasantly tired from swimming laps and sitting in the sun, and examined her closet for something to wear. Isabella stretched luxuriously on the bed where she lay in a small circle of sunshine, and Rebecca laughed softly. Everyone's mood had been elevated by the weather, and she herself felt very content. Of course she didn't have anything wonderful to wear, but that was not unexpected, and it didn't disturb her.

Tucked away in the back of the closet, however, she did find a soft sleeveless white dress with a few splashes of large yellow flowers, and she remembered that she even had some matching enameled earrings to wear. It had been steaming hot down on the peninsula, and it seemed unlikely that it would be much cooler by dinnertime, so the dress would be ideal. It was one she didn't wear much, since it was usually too summery for San Francisco at any time of the year.

She showered, realizing after she turned the water on that it was her third shower of the day. She certainly wouldn't be the most beautiful date Jared had ever had, or the most sexually sophisticated, but she would probably be the cleanest, she told herself as she wiped the steam from her mirror. Her hair brushed easily into a loose knot at the top of her head, which kept it off her neck, and she examined her face critically, noticing that her nose was a little pink from sunburn. She was happy to discover that the dress looked better than she had expected. It flowed softly around her bare legs and clung to her breasts, and as she put on her pale yellow sandals, she decided that all things considered, she looked just fine.

She fed the cats and somehow left the house a little late, already feeling the anticipation of Jared's presence. *None of that,* she reminded herself as she felt her heart begin to beat a little faster. If they still liked each other, if this evening went well, there would be plenty of time later for the satisfaction of her burgeoning physical desires.

Where had they come from, anyway, these intense, demanding needs that had recently occupied so much of her attention? It wasn't just that she'd been alone for a year. She'd been alone for many years before she got involved with Ed. It was something about Jared, his gentleness and consideration, that had opened a reservoir of sensuality she'd kept locked inside her, hidden from herself as much as from anyone else. Thinking about it even in such an abstract way seemed to alter the chemistry of her body, causing her breath to come faster, her face to flush, and she leaned back a little into the leather seat, wishing she had a tape of sultry love songs to play.

As she exited from the freeway, she automatically began paying more attention to her surroundings, remembering Jared's directions. His house was only a few miles from her office, so she was familiar with the area, but she didn't think she'd ever been anywhere in west Atherton before. As far as she knew, there were very few houses there that you could buy for less than half a million dollars, and many cost considerably more. Accordingly, her friends lived in other communities.

Somewhat tentatively she turned onto the broad, tree-lined street that he'd said would lead to his house. The leaves on the tall, flaring oak trees seemed to hang limply in the still air, and even the pine trees were drooping. Sprinklers were on everywhere, and there still wasn't a cloud in the sky or a sign of fog on the horizon.

She turned up a steep hill onto a road lined with tall, spindly eucalyptus trees and began looking for his house. Her heart was beating a little faster than usual. She could feel the flush in her cheeks, and even knowing how much she wanted to see him, she was a little surprised at her sense of excitement as she found the number on Jared's mailbox and turned. The narrow driveway led steeply downhill and around a curve. Then she saw the house, which seemed to proceed down the hill over several terraces.

There was enough room in the driveway to park several cars, so she picked a spot near the front door and stopped in front of the low concrete barrier that prevented cars from rolling into the bushes and down the steep hillside. The house was white and had a large double door in front, between banks of square-paned windows surrounded by shrubbery. A wooden stairway circled down the far left side before disappearing in the oleanders, and she guessed it led to another entrance.

She lifted the knocker at the front and gave a timid rap, then lifted it again for a more hefty crack. Within seconds she heard footsteps approaching on the other side of the door, and her heart seemed to catch in her throat and make her breathless. Then Jared was in the doorway, smiling, wearing light gray slacks and a thin cotton blue-and-white-striped shirt. His hair seemed even curlier than usual, and she wanted to touch it, to smooth it over his forehead and down the back of his neck. Instead she just smiled back and said "Hi."

Jared opened the door farther and ushered her into the hall, amazed that she could seem so cool on such a wilting hot day. He himself had just climbed out of the pool in time to light the charcoal. As he closed the door behind them, he looked at her more closely. He liked her hair up on top of her head. It was sexy somehow, giving him the feeling that he could just remove one or two pins and all her glowing, autumn-colored hair would tumble down around her shoulders. When she smiled he wanted to kiss her, but it seemed presumptuous somehow.

"I wish I'd told you to bring your swimsuit," he said, putting one tentative hand on her shoulder to lead her across the living room and through the sliding glass doors to the patio. "I have a pool, and it's very refreshing on days like this."

When she laughed, he realized he'd almost forgotten what a wonderful, husky laugh she had. It matched her voice perfectly. "I've already done my laps today," she said. "I'll be happy just to sit in a shady spot somewhere with a cool drink."

"Would a vodka collins be okay?"

"Wonderful," she answered, "if it's very light on the vodka."

He guided her to the stairs that led down to the pool, admiring the way her rich brown hair shone as she descended. He had the charcoal lighted and everything ready in the little pool-house refrigerator. The white wrought-iron table was set up at the side of the pool house, in a little alcove created by the trees at the corner of his yard. It was cool there in the shade, away from the glare coming off the water.

She sat down gracefully, the white skirt exposing barely a centimeter of her knees, and Jared went into the pool house to get their drinks. She was so lovely he was going to have a hard time keeping his hands off her until later in the evening.

"Here's to second dates," he said, handing her a glass, and her eyebrows rose a little.

"I remember you had some generalizations to make about first dates. Is there any special reason to toast second dates?" She flushed a little, realizing that she might have sounded snide, and she tried to make a recovery by adding, "Beyond the fact that this is our second date."

"Second dates are crucial, I think. They come when a relationship is still very fragile—anything can disrupt it. So if you'd tripped on the steps and broken your arm, or if I'd spilled your drink all over your lap, that would have meant the end of everything, even though those same things would be trivial later on in a relationship."

Rebecca pursed her lips. "I hardly think of breaking my arm as trivial." She cocked her head a little, looking at him very seriously. "Now if it were *your* arm, that might be trivial."

He laughed, taking a sip of his drink and enjoying her mischievous smile. She had a whole repertoire of smiles, it seemed, some with dimples and some without, and they all made her beautiful. A patch of sunlight was glinting on her calf, which was smooth and lightly tanned. He'd love to run his hands up over the firm muscle to the softer flesh above her knees, to stroke the warm, tender skin while he kissed her. He took a long breath and resolved to think about something very impersonal for a few minutes.

"It sounds to me as if your dates have been fraught with mishaps," Rebecca said, and he shrugged.

"I've had my share of disasters," he said. "Once when I was trying to be very suave, the door handle fell off my car onto the road when I closed the door. And once," he went on, "I went through an entire evening with a poisonous green spot in the middle of my tie."

"And were those both second dates?"

"Last dates," he said, reaching to touch the bare skin of her forearm.

"By comparison, things seem to be going rather smoothly for us. Of course, you did burn your hand last time. . . ."

Jared rolled his eyes. "You would remember that as the most significant event of the evening. Haven't you had any memorable disasters on other dates?"

She thought for a moment. "Not really, but then I've probably had fewer dates than you."

His eyes met hers. "What makes you say that?"

"I guess because there have been periods in my life when I haven't dated. My work is very important to me, and often it consumes so much of my time I haven't been able to do much else." She paused. "I suppose that sounds strange to you."

"A little. I don't think I've ever known a woman who was so involved in her profession, so you're quite a new experience for me."

Rebecca frowned a little, then grinned. "Maybe I'm not your type," she said lightly.

He put his hand over hers and leaned across the table. "I'm sure that's not true," he said. "Maybe it's the others who aren't my type."

The others. It was easy to imagine them—sophisticated, experienced, a little frivolous. But she wouldn't waste her energy being jealous of the past if she could be sure everyone else really was in the past. It was much too soon to ask Jared about that, she knew.

A little reluctantly Jared pushed his chair back. "I'd better check the dinner."

Rebecca stayed at the table, her hand wrapped lightly around the cool glass. The birds were singing gaily in the oak trees, and it was very relaxing at Jared's house. No hustle-and-bustle city noises, or the sounds of barking dogs and throbbing lawnmowers she usually associated with suburbia. The air was still and quiet enough to encourage daydreams, so she watched the play of shadows on the grass and remembered how Jared had made her feel the last time they'd been together at her house.

When he came back he was carrying two cold asparagus salads, and Rebecca began to suspect that she could never invite him over to dinner.

"If your cooking is too much better than mine," she told him, "I won't be able to endure the humiliation of cooking for you."

"I have a secret passion for frozen pot pies," he assured her, "so don't worry."

They looked at each other for a few seconds, a look that Rebecca found so charged with emotion that she had to drop her eyes and concentrate on her salad. Too much was happening too soon, and she could feel herself beginning to stiffen up. It was frightening to recognize the intensity of the contact between them,

83

the buildup of sexual tension. She felt short of breath and wondered if she'd be able to eat much of her dinner.

The next course—filet mignon, baked potato, and fresh peas—was exquisitely cooked. At her house the filets would have been overcooked, the potatoes half raw, and the peas boiled to a sodden mass. Still, it was rather typical male fare, better than if he'd served her veal Oscar or pork chops stuffed with wild rice. She ate slowly, still feeling nervous anticipation, and she was grateful that by some miracle their conversation seemed to flow smoothly, as if she were completely relaxed.

By the time they finished it was nearly dark, and a stiff breeze had come up that promised to bring in cool ocean air to end the day's heat.

"I think we can go inside now," Jared said, "if we open everything up and I turn on the attic fan. Then I can show you a few slides."

"I'll do the dishes while you're getting things ready," Rebecca offered as she stood up, but Jared shook his head and stacked several of the earthenware plates in his arms.

"I'll put them in the dishwasher right now if you insist, but I'd rather just stack them in the sink and worry about them tomorrow."

"Don't you hate waking up to a sink full of dirty dishes?" she asked. "I do."

"I think you're much more organized than I am, much neater," he said, giving her a measuring look. He smiled suddenly. "I'm learning a few things about you, and I'd like to know more."

They were in the house, and Jared had put the dishes down with an alarming clatter. He looked at Rebecca for a minute, then gave another, different kind of smile that immediately heated her blood.

"Why don't you sit down comfortably somewhere and look at photographs for a few minutes?"

With a warm hand on her elbow, he ushered her into the living room, which she now looked at closely for the first time. It was decorated very simply, with wood and leather furniture and glass-top tables.

A beige-carpeted hall led off to the side of the room, beyond the glass doors. Presumably the bedrooms were in that direction. The living room windows that faced the driveway were partially shrouded by shrubbery, so that even in the daytime it probably wasn't possible to see the road from inside. Now that night had almost fallen, the leaves gave the room a cozy, sheltered feeling, avoiding the sensation of a waiting black abyss usually created by uncurtained windows in the dark. There was a bookshelf next to the large stone fireplace, and there she saw several silver tea glass holders that she thought might have come from Nepal. There were a few other things, too—a photograph of a young girl who was probably Jared's sister, an antique oil lamp, a cloisonné vase, and a huge sea urchin.

She sat down on the tan leather sofa, and Jared handed her a gold-embossed red leather album bound at the side with a red silk cord. "I bought this in Nepal, for my best shots." He opened it gently, and she saw that each page had a protective lining of rice paper. "This will explain why I wanted to live there," he said. "If you want to see more after this, then I'll put up the screen for slides."

He left the room again, and she heard occasional thumps of windows and doors opening as she examined the photographs. The scenery was really too spectacular to seem real, she thought. The shots of round-faced children made it easier for her to imagine herself there, but even so it seemed very exotic, a land seen only in pictures and never to be experienced in reality. The rings of mist that obscured the mountain peaks made Nepal look like a fantasy land.

There were three pictures of a woman whom Rebecca immediately identified as someone Jared had been involved with. Her poses were polished, like a fashion model's, and her clothes were beautiful. In one picture she stood on some ancient stone steps, wearing a stylish blue dress and a broad-brimmed hat. Her elfin features and short black hair showed plainly, and Rebecca gave a tiny sigh. Surely the glamorous woman in the picture was Jared's type, not a serious psychologist like herself. She closed the album quickly when she heard Jared's footsteps leaving the kitchen.

"Why aren't there any shots of you in here?" she asked when he reappeared. "That would make a magical place like Nepal seem more real."

His eyes narrowed. "I hate shots of people standing in front of this or that, obscuring all the best scenery." He sat down next to her, and for the first time that evening she smelled the faint leathery scent of his aftershave. "I'm a little sorry that I won't be spending long periods of time there anymore, although I will be going back once or twice a year."

"It sounds as if you really like being there," she commented.

"In many ways. I went there several years ago on a vacation—a walking tour. It's an impoverished country, but beautiful and with a simplicity we can't even imagine here. So I went back, again and again, and then some colleagues went with me, and gradually I realized that I could improve conditions there a little and become self-employed at the same time. Those have long been two dreams of mine." He smiled at her somewhat tentatively, as if he'd revealed more than he'd intended.

86

"What made you come back?" she asked, secretly glad his long stays in Nepal had ended.

He leaned comfortably against the sofa. "Someone has to keep an eye on the market, make sure we're planning to produce what people will be wanting in the future. I happen to have a gift for predicting market trends, just as you have a gift for helping troubled people."

She looked at him very seriously. "Sometimes I'm not sure I have a gift," she said, and then for some reason she found herself telling him about the father she'd scared off with her self-righteous anger. As she talked, he listened intently, his eyes never leaving her face. The way he gave her his undivided attention seemed to make it easier for her to open up to him and express her guilt and self-doubts. Tears burned her eyes for an instant, and he took her hand between his, still looking at her.

"None of us is perfect," he said very gently. "You have to expect to make a mistake now and then."

Rebecca shook her head. "It wasn't just a mistake, as if I'd tried something that didn't work. It was that I didn't do my job. I thought of myself instead of him."

"And do you plan to forgive yourself for that lapse?" he asked.

Rebecca was quiet. Jared hadn't belittled her feelings of failure; he had listened to her with more understanding than she would have expected. And because of that she felt much closer to him now. She felt she could be honest with him, knowing he would listen to what she said.

"I've never been very good at forgiving myself," she admitted, looking straight into the gray depths of his eyes.

"Oh, Rebecca," he said softly, lifting her hand to his lips. There was a faint smile on his face, as if he knew and accepted all her foibles, as if he would soothe all her fears and worries.

She leaned toward him and his arms were around her, one hand on the back of her neck to turn her mouth toward his. She succumbed easily to the gentle pressure of his fingers, her lips meeting his softly as his thumb moved up and down the nape of her neck. His lips were warm and tasted faintly of wine. She licked gently at the entrance to his mouth, wanting to prolong their kiss indefinitely. She would savor every instant, each breath and heartbeat, and then . . .

Her mind refused to contemplate any abrupt end to the embrace, but she found it equally difficult to plan deliberately on making love with Jared. Languidly she traced his ear with one finger, her tongue still teasing him. For once she'd have to take each moment as it came, without mapping out her whole future. It was time to enjoy her feelings, to let go of her inhibitions. She didn't pretend that she was in love with Jared, or that he loved her, but they certainly liked each other. At the moment all that mattered was the warmth of his body, the memory of his compassion, the exciting pressure of his mouth.

She stroked his cheek with the tips of her fingers. Jared's hand on her neck grew more insistent, and she knew he wanted a fuller kiss. Still she withheld her tongue, moving her lips tantalizingly against his, enjoying the prickle of his mustache against her upper lip as she moved her head slightly left and right.

Jared's other arm tightened around her waist and suddenly their tongues met, flicking gently at each other. She slid her hand down his neck to his chest, where she felt his heart pounding against her palm. She withdrew her tongue, knowing his would follow, and then released a long breath as his gentle tickling exploration of her mouth began. His tongue stroked the sensitive area inside her lips, then moved softly against the top of her own tongue as her hand moved eagerly up and down his chest. She felt his muscles, his ribs, the hollow of his shoulder, and always she was aware of his strong, fierce heartbeat and his ever-deepening breathing.

Her own pulses were racing. Her skin was warm and eager, but somehow she felt no sense of haste. She was quite content to learn every ridge and hollow of his chest, to experience the soft quest of his tongue. She would stay in his arms all night, floating on a warm, gentle sea of tender caresses. She opened her eyes for an instant and looked at him, charmed by the long brown lashes that curled up from his eyelids. When she saw only his closed eyes, he seemed young and vulnerable, completely intent on their kiss.

His eyes opened then, dark with passion, and he smiled at her, stroking her cheek with gentle fingers. "This is very nice," he said softly. "All evening I've wanted to be closer to you, to show you how I feel about you." He kissed her very lightly. "I don't want to move too fast for you, so be sure to tell me if I am." He looked at her for a moment, and she shook her head.

Maybe too much was happening too quickly, but this tender closeness was too important to interrupt. Without speaking, they were learning to know and trust each other. "I think it's a good idea to express what we're feeling," she said, surprised to hear how husky her voice was. "I'm enjoying it, too . . . very much."

"Good," he said, and bent to kiss her again.

One of her arms was trapped against the sofa and she shifted to free it, then curled it under his arm and up so she could caress the back of his neck.

His left arm slid across her back, and then with a

faint sigh she felt his fingers stroke the sensitive skin of her inner arm and rub the inside of her forearm, not softly enough to tickle her but still tenderly. Caressing his tongue with hers, she pushed a little closer to him so her breasts were crushed against his chest. His hand drifted upward to her shoulder and massaged it, his thumb rubbing along the hollow near her neck.

Her skin was very soft against the palm of his hand. He wished she were naked, so that he could stroke her spine, explore the edges of her ribs beneath the smooth, faintly perfumed skin. At the thought his breath came faster and his hand tightened on her shoulder.

He remembered feeling the zipper at the back of her dress and wondered if he could unzip it just far enough to bare her shoulders completely. He wanted her, but it was too soon. What they had now was far too good to risk losing, and he could feel in her warm but somehow languid response to him that she wasn't ready to make love. She was enjoying the slow heat of this gentle closeness, and so was he. But he wouldn't be able to sit there for long without wanting more. His need for her was growing by the minute, and soon it would overpower his restraint.

Carefully he pulled away a little, caressing her cheek with his fingertips. "Let's go have our coffee out by the pool," he said huskily. "It's getting too hot in here."

"All right." She sat up somewhat dazedly, smoothing her dress down over her knees, and smiling at him. "Cool air might just be what we both need right now."

Jared kept his opinion of what they both needed right now to himself, and led the way into the kitchen, where he poured two mugs of coffee from the pot he'd prepared earlier. As they walked to the pool, Rebecca shivered. It was quite a bit cooler outside.

"I forgot to turn on the pool light," Jared said, and turned back to the house to flick a switch. A soft light beamed up through the turquoise water, barely illuminating the area around the pool, and Rebecca saw for the first time a picnic table and benches just around the corner of the pool. She began to walk toward it, being careful not to spill her coffee. The heel of her sandal twisted in a concrete joint and she stumbled against Jared, who stepped away quickly to avoid the hot coffee spilling out of her tilted mug.

There was a healthy splash as he landed in the pool, his mug still level as he disappeared under the water. "Oh, my God! Jared!" Rebecca shouted, putting her mug down and kicking off her shoes. But then Jared surfaced, his hair plastered to his forehead, his shirt clinging to his shoulders. Treading water, he lifted his mug to his lips and took a dignified sip.

"It's not the best coffee I ever made," he said with a straight face. Rebecca burst out laughing.

"You can have what's left of mine," she said. "That's only fair."

"You have a wonderful laugh," he said, climbing out of the pool.

He looked ridiculous. He looked wonderful with his wet clothes clinging to him, water running down his arms, splashing onto the concrete. But Rebecca stopped laughing when they stood only a few feet apart and looked at each other.

"So much for second dates," she said softly. She felt a little breathless, and she didn't think the sensation was caused by her laughter.

"Maybe we can still salvage this one," Jared said, moving a little closer to her. "But first, there's something I must know."

"What?" she asked, trying to imagine what could be so urgent.

"Is that dress washable?"

Her eyes widened. Surely he wouldn't throw her in the pool. "I'm not sure," she hedged.

He moved still nearer. "Let's live dangerously, then." His arms went around her shoulders, cold and wet, and he pulled her close. As their lips met, she was briefly aware of a chilly feeling from his wet clothes. Then the sudden rush of her heart at the sensation of his mustache against her upper lip made her forget everything but how much she wanted him. His tongue moved more forcefully than before, and his hands were more demanding as they moved down her back to cup her buttocks. He seemed to lift her as he pressed her against him, his embrace insisting that she recognize their mutual need.

She arched her back, pressing her body against the very satisfying evidence of his arousal, and her hips rocked against him in an age-old involuntary rhythm as she clutched at his back, suddenly too caught up in her own urgency to tolerate any delays. She had wanted him earlier, but without this frantic necessity. Now she felt feverish with desire. She ran her hands down his back, smoothing the wet shirt against his skin as she caressed him. She filled his mouth with her tongue, wanting him to know that for now she was his, and would withhold nothing. Her breasts were aching, longing to be touched, and she almost sobbed as his fingers slid up her inner thighs until they aroused her at the center of her femininity.

"Maybe you should get out of these wet clothes," she murmured against his lips. "It would be a pity if you caught a cold."

He kissed the corner of her mouth, her cheek, then her ear before replying in a voice that was suddenly very deep. "What a good idea." His hands moved again, stroking up her back, then moving under her

92

arms to cup and gently lift her breasts. "You've gotten wet, too," he said as she leaned against him, pressing his hands between her breasts and his chest.

His fingers found the tab to her zipper and then in an instant she felt him unhook her bra. His hands were very warm against the exposed skin of her back as he pulled sleeves and straps forward and down her arms in one easy movement. Then his hands were on her breasts again, the center of his palms against her nipples, and she moaned softly and began to work at the buttons of his shirt. The fabric was wet and resistant, and the circling movements of his hands made it hard to concentrate.

His hands left her breasts suddenly and then she was being lifted, carried through the sliding doors, and deposited gently on the soft padded carpeting in the living room. They both worked buttons and zippers with intense concentration, sometimes undressing themselves and sometimes each other, concerned only with removing the barriers between them. Then at last they were naked in the dark and he was on his knees beside her, his hands tracing the flare of her hips and the soft curve of her breast against her ribs.

"Your skin is so smooth," he said. "It's wonderful to touch."

She was looking up at him, her golden eyes gleaming, and he put one hand in her hair to find the pins that fastened it. Her hands clutched at his arms and he leaned over to kiss her very softly. It wasn't right to rush this, no matter how feverish they had been a moment ago. So he stroked her hair, calming her until he felt her body begin to relax. "We have all the time in the world," he told her, carefully smoothing her delicate eyebrows. Her lips were parted, her breath still came quickly, and as he looked at her he felt a rush of elation. She was so beautiful, her tan skin soft and unlined, the white patches left by her swimsuit gleaming enticingly.

He had pulled her hair loose and it spread around her head, its color rich against the pale carpet. It fell sleekly between his fingers, the strands slipping from his grasp as he lifted them. Her fingers moved delicately down his chest and brushed his stomach before they moved up and around his waist. She was tugging him toward her and he complied, sliding down so that his mouth covered the rosy tip of one breast. She gasped as he flicked her nipple with his tongue, and he put one hand on her hipbone, pressing her gently into the carpet as she twisted against him.

His mouth moved from her breasts down the smooth cool skin of her stomach and into the warmth beyond. She pulled away at first, trying to lift him away from her, and he murmured something to her soothingly, stroking her legs until he felt her relax. She moaned, her fingers clenched in his hair, and he lifted one hand to her breast and carefully stroked her nipple until she cried out and arched her back.

Waves of sensation rushed through her body, then slowly diminished as he slid upward and took her in his arms as gently as if she might shatter. She turned on her side and pressed against him, wanting more even as she marveled at the sensations he had so easily aroused. She felt the hardness of his shoulder and the furred skin of his arm as he planted small kisses in the hollow of her neck. His eyes were very dark, almost black, when she looked at him, and she smiled, rolling over to her back and pulling him after her.

A lock of hair had fallen over his forehead and she brushed it away tenderly, looking up at him as he seemed to hesitate. She had the luxury of time now that her terrible urgency had been satisfied, and she ran her hands lightly down his back and over his buttocks, then lifted her hips to meet him and enclose him.

He kissed her, moving gently against her, and she explored his back with her fingers. By slow degrees she felt him enter her and then she lay still for a moment, caressing him softly until his thrusts became less gentle. Then suddenly her own urgency seemed to match his and she gasped, gripping his buttocks to press him to her more tightly.

Pulsating sensations began to spread down her legs and over her stomach and she opened herself completely, moaning as the fire took control of her. She said his name and immediately felt him drive even deeper, his mouth searching for her nipple. He made a low, harsh sound and she wrapped her arms around him tightly as his movements gradually ceased.

He propped himself on his elbows and smiled down at her, tiny drops of perspiration gleaming on his forehead. "Was I too rough?" he asked, and she shook her head, surprised. It seemed to her that he had been very gentle.

"I didn't want to hurt you," he said, combing her hair with the fingers of one hand.

"You didn't hurt me," she told him, shaking her head again. "Quite the contrary."

"Good." He relaxed his arms and lay down, most of his weight on the rug next to her. "I don't ever want to hurt you."

What made him say that? she wondered. Could he already sense her heightened vulnerability to him? Or was she reading things into a straightforward statement? Sometimes she caught herself overanalyzing things.

She turned her head a little to look at him, and smiled to herself. His eyes were closed, their long lashes curling up, and she felt very protective, wondering if he was sleeping. He opened his eyes and leaned over to kiss her.

"Is there anyone else right now?" he asked.

"There hasn't been anyone for quite a while," she said, then hesitated. "What about you?"

He laughed a little. "I just got back from Nepal, where my social life was limited, to say the least."

She could ask him now about the woman in the pictures, but she decided against it. There'd be time later to satisfy her curiosity.

"Would you like some tea, or mineral water?" he asked.

"Sure. I'll have whatever you're having."

He sat up, holding out his hands to her. "Come on up to my bedroom. My bed is a lot more comfortable than the floor," he said, grinning. "We can have our drinks there. And I'll bring the dessert, too."

She started to pick up her clothes, but he shook his head. "Don't worry about that now. It's too warm inside to put anything on."

His bedroom was almost aggressively masculine, she thought, with navy blue pin-striped bedding and a navy blue armchair in the corner. After turning on one dim light, he pulled back the sheets and set a blue corduroy backrest on one side of the bed for her. She sat down there, pulling the sheet up to her waist, and he bent forward to kiss her.

"I'll be back in two minutes," he said.

The queen-size bed had a bookcase headboard that was stacked with magazines, and she leafed through them curiously. They were all computer journals, nothing that she would be interested in reading. As she restacked them, Jared appeared with a tray.

"I decided on iced tea and chocolate mousse," he said, carefully placing the tray across her knees and sitting down next to her.

96

"Mmmm." She looked over at him, surprised that she could feel so comfortable sitting in bed with him. Everything had seemed so easy, so right. Even now she wasn't particularly self-conscious. She took the last bite of mousse and put the tray on a low table beside the bed. When she turned back, Jared was looking at her, his face close to hers.

"I knew we'd be good together," he said. He bent to kiss the very tip of one breast, then glanced up at her quickly. "Or am I taking too much for granted?"

Rebecca wrinkled her nose. "Is this false modesty?"

"Not really." He sat back against his pillow and folded his arms around his knees. "Some women pretend, you know. I flatter myself that I can tell, but I wanted to make sure." He kissed the top of her other breast, but for the moment her mind was elsewhere.

"Have there been lots of women?" she asked finally, feeling sure that there had been.

"I've known several women. More than several," he said slowly. "Does that bother you?"

"A little," she admitted. "I don't like being part of a crowd."

He sat up again, his knees drawn close together. "Nothing lasts forever, we both know that. But that doesn't make what you and I have together right now any less valuable, does it?"

"I suppose not. But everything happened so fast, at least by my standards."

"Rebecca, I like you a lot. You're a very special woman to me. I thought that was pretty obvious," he said, sounding surprised. "I feel as if I've known you much longer than I really have, and I'd assumed you felt the same way." He smiled a little. "You're very serious about everything, aren't you? How did you end up in bed with someone who makes such terrible puns?"

Rebecca shrugged. "Chance? A twist of fate? Destiny?"

"Ah, destiny. Never fight destiny . . ." He was kissing her breasts again, and it was difficult for her to think about anything but the delicious sensations his tongue was provoking.

She slid down on the bed until they were side by side. Her blood was racing already as his fingers brushed lightly over her skin. She put her hands on either side of his face and kissed him luxuriously, pressing her full length against him. When she heard him inhale sharply, she smiled a little, her hands moving playfully down his back to his thighs. She caressed him delicately as their kiss became harder, then curled her legs around him.

Once again they were joined, and this time her response was startlingly immediate. She gripped his shoulders, gasping, while her body trembled uncontrollably. She lost all sense of the separateness of their bodies as the dizzying swells of pleasure seemed to lift her into a world completely devoted to sensation. When Jared groaned and lightly bit the tendon of her neck, she gave an exultant cry and fell back against the bed.

She'd never let herself go so completely, she thought a few seconds later as Jared turned out the light and covered her lightly with a sheet. Not with Ed, although he'd said that he loved her. Why, then, was it happening so easily with Jared? Explanations chased each other briefly in her thoughts as she snuggled close to him, her back against his chest. His arm was warm around her and the pillow was soft. Within seconds she was sound asleep, safe and warm in his bed.

CHAPTER SIX

Rebecca dreamed she was walking through a warm, heavily shaded forest. Birds were singing loudly. They were blackbirds, she decided, recognizing the shrill, sweet notes. A stream was coursing nearby, and a voice was saying, "Do you jog?" She decided to ignore the voice.

"Do you jog?" the voice said again, and she felt a hand on her shoulder.

"Mmmph," she responded, and pulled the striped sheet over her head.

"I'll be back in an hour," the voice persisted. "Don't say I didn't invite you."

She was aware of various household noises, culminating in the click of a door closing, and suddenly she was awake. Slowly she lowered the sheet and looked around Jared's bedroom, now lit with sunlight filtered through lowered blue Roman shades. She could hardly have gone jogging in her dress and sandals, anyway, she realized as soon as her mind began to work, so why had Jared asked her? She sincerely hoped that he didn't have a collection of women's shorts, tops, and running shoes for the convenience of his overnight guests. As she had told him last night, she had no interest in being one of a crowd.

What she should do, she decided, was get dressed. She peered down the hall, noting that the doors and windows seemed to be closed, and darted into the living room to retrieve her clothes. For some reason she felt as if someone were going to come in at any moment and discover her naked in the living room—probably just the effect of being alone in a strange house. Jared had folded her things and stacked them neatly on a chair, and he'd even brought her shoes in from the pool. Gratefully she gathered up the bundle and hurried back down the hall in search of a shower.

The bathroom off Jared's bedroom seemed her best choice, and she noticed a clean set of towels draped invitingly over a rack next to the sink. The room itself was pale blue, the towels white with one satiny blue stripe, and Jared's terry-cloth bathrobe, which hung on a hook behind the door, was a startling bright orange. How nice that everything wasn't matching, she thought as she scrubbed diligently in the shower. She had begun to feel that Jared was a little too perfect, at least in his decorating habits.

She dressed quickly, grateful that the knit dress wasn't too wrinkled, and pulled her shampooed hair back with a clip she kept in her purse. Then she sat down in the living room and leafed through the morning newspaper she found lying on the floor at the front door.

It was uncomfortable, being alone in Jared's house, and she found it hard to concentrate on the newspaper. To be left by herself, after what had happened last night, wasn't very reassuring. She was tempted to go home right now, but it would be rude to leave without saying good-bye to Jared first.

He opened the front door several minutes later, flushed and perspiring in green running shorts and a white T-shirt. His legs were long and slender, and nicely hairy above his white socks. When he caught sight of her he grinned and walked over to kiss her lightly.

"I had some idea of climbing back into bed with you," he told her, "but I guess I missed my chance."

Rebecca smiled back. It was good to see him, but she was still a little hurt that he had gone off so casually. "It's time for me to go," she said. "I was just waiting to say good-bye."

He stood there for a moment, looking at her, and then he frowned. "I should have stayed here with you this morning." He sat down next to her on the sofa, careful to leave a little distance between them. "I'm not usually so inconsiderate. It just seemed so natural, waking up with you next to me, that I acted as if I'd known you for months." He looked at her very seriously. "I'd like you to stay and have some breakfast, so we can talk. If you leave now . . ." He made an upward gesture with his hands. "Will you stay?"

"All right."

"I'll just pour us some coffee," he said, standing again.

He was back within minutes and set two mugs on the table next to her, then sat down and put his arm lightly around her shoulders.

"I guess things went too fast," Rebecca said immediately. "Now I'm uncomfortable."

He tightened his arm around her, then released it. "I know everything happened more quickly than we expected," he said. "Maybe if I tell you how I feel about it, it will help you feel better."

She nodded, and he took her hand with his free one. "I'm very intensely attracted to you," he said. "Unusually so. And I'd like to get to know you much better. I think we can have some very nice times together, if we just take it step by step. Is that something you'd like also?"

"The thing is . . ." she began, and he sat up a little straighter. She seemed to be struggling to find words, and he squeezed her hand to encourage her a little.

"I'm quite monogamous," she said finally. "And if you're going to be seeing other women," she gestured vaguely toward the bedroom, "I'd like to know that right now."

"I think I've always been monogamous too," he said, pulling her a little closer. "While you and I are seeing each other regularly, you can be sure I won't be getting involved with anyone else. Okay?"

"Fine," she agreed with a shy smile.

He pulled her toward him and their lips met, causing an immediate response in Rebecca's body. Her skin flushed, her breasts felt swollen and heavy, and she sighed, caressing the back of his head. Reluctantly he pulled away, kissing her quickly on the nose.

"You're all clean and I'm sweaty," he said. "Of course, we could change all that."

Rebecca hesitated, pulling away a little. She was happy now, relieved by his assurance that he felt the same way about their relationship that she did. But she didn't want to confine what was growing between them to the bedroom.

"Or maybe I could fix some breakfast," he said, standing up. "How do you like your eggs?"

"Any way at all, as long as they are cooked by someone other than me," Rebecca said, laughing and carrying their coffee cups into the kitchen.

"Would you like me to shower first, or do you think you can stand to sit at the table with me?" Jared asked.

"Don't shower on my account." She smiled. Actually, she liked the way he smelled—very masculine and kind of musky—and it made her feel closer to him to be able to have breakfast with him when he was all sweaty and his hair was all mussed up.

There were benches built into a corner of the kitchen, with a square butcher-block table in front of them, and she slid behind the table, admiring his technique as he rapidly sliced a handful of mushrooms.

"How about a mushroom and sour cream omelet?" he asked, and she nearly laughed, thinking of what she would have cooked for herself this morning.

"That sounds wonderful."

"I'm a little out of practice," he said, beating a little cream into several eggs. "I didn't cook in Nepal, because my housekeeper there felt cooking was her exclusive territory. So now I'm enjoying the luxury of being able to eat exactly what I want when I want it."

Rebecca took another sip of coffee and stretched her legs under the table. The deep aroma of the coffee, the smell of eggs cooking in butter, the sound of birds singing—all seemed extraordinarily vivid. All her senses had been awakened by Jared's lovemaking. With her heightened awareness she could feel the soft fabric of her dress everywhere it touched her skin. She was aware of the rough feel of the nubby fabric that covered the bench she sat on, the smooth coolness of the wooden table leg her sandaled foot was brushing. Even her still-damp hair resting against her neck seemed particularly heavy.

Her taste buds also shared in this new world of sensation, she discovered as Jared sat down and she tasted her omelet. Either that or Jared was a world-class chef. In either case, she had devoured everything on her plate before she noticed that Jared had eaten less than half of his.

"Very good," she told him, and he gave a dry smile.

"Apparently. Would you like another?"

"Probably not." She took a deep breath, enjoying

the feeling of fullness. "I'm not really that hungry. I just made a pig of myself because it tasted so good."

"When we talk," Jared said suddenly, putting down his fork, "it's usually about me. I'd like to learn some things about you, too."

She smiled. "Anything you'd like to know, just ask me."

He thought for a moment. "Okay. Do you like to travel?"

"I don't really know," she said. "I've been to Canada and New England, and that's about it. Sometimes there are conferences in faraway places like Paris or Tokyo and I think about going, but I'm always too busy."

"What do you do for fun?" he asked, and she shrugged.

"I swim, I see friends, occasionally I go to the movies."

He grinned. "Maybe I can add a little frivolity to your life. Or are you too ambitious to relax for long?"

Rebecca was a little surprised. "I've never really thought of myself as being ambitious," she said. "I did set some goals for myself, but I've achieved them now." She frowned. "Do you think I'm a workaholic?"

He shook his head. "No, just a little too dedicated, maybe. Or maybe not. I could tell when I met you that you were devoted to your work. That's one of the things that attracted me, I think, and it's certainly why I wanted you to see Meredith."

"How is your sister?"

"I think she's doing all right. Certainly she's not getting any worse," he said quietly.

After they'd discussed Meredith's progress, Rebecca felt that it was time to head home. To her, last night had been such an overwhelming experience that it seemed as if her whole life had changed. Since meeting Jared she'd begun to see herself differently. She was more of a sensual being than she'd ever thought, and while that came as a surprise, it was a nice one. As a psychologist, she'd always wondered a little about her rather celibate life. She knew the causes for it—she was very busy and she rarely met men she was attracted to and trusted. The question, of course, was always why it didn't bother her more that she wasn't having sex. And the answer was obviously that she hadn't known what she was missing.

Jared, on the other hand, had dated many women. With all his experience he'd be much better able to take his relationship with her in stride. She needed to make sure she kept her feelings enough in check that she wouldn't find herself wanting much more from him than he was willing to give.

"You're a very good cook," she told him as she stood up. "The dinner and the breakfast were delicious, and I've had a wonderful time being with you. But now I think I should go home and get myself organized for next week."

He looked at her for a moment, a faint frown hinting that perhaps she was rushing off a little precipitously. "All right," he said eventually. "When shall we get together again?"

Keep it cool, she reminded herself. *Don't rush things.* "How about next weekend?"

"All right," he said again. "Would you like to go for a hike, say on Saturday afternoon, and then have dinner later?"

"Sounds good to me." She smiled, feeling quite happy. She had a lovely day to look forward to, and she'd protected herself reasonably well from getting overinvolved with him. If they saw each other only once a week, she would easily be able to live her own life and concentrate on her work, as if Jared didn't even exist. Then when she did see him, it would be a delightful interlude, like a brief vacation.

She walked around the table to him, smiling, and he stood up and held his arms out. "You don't have to leave so soon, do you?" He pulled her close, and she felt the regular beat of his heart beneath his T-shirt. She laid her head against his shoulder for a moment, enjoying the tickle of his mustache against her neck.

"I really do have to," she murmured, lifting her head to brush her lips against his.

His arms tightened around her as his lips pressed more firmly against hers. Again her body responded as if by magic, and she pulled away half reluctantly. "I'd better go right now," she said, and he released her.

They walked together to her car, and as she opened the door, he kissed her on the cheek. "I'll call you later in the week and we can decide on a time," he said as she climbed in. " 'Bye."

She pulled out of the driveway quickly, feeling a little sad at saying good-bye. Now she regretted the week that would elapse before she saw Jared again. All the more reason to stick to her resolution, she decided. If it was hard to say good-bye after only one night together, it would be much harder after longer or more frequent meetings. She would have to get used to these small partings, and perhaps that would prepare her for the big parting that was bound to come later on.

She slipped into her garage, wanting to keep everything very much to herself. Right now her relationship with Jared seemed much too important and too new to discuss with Madeleine or anyone else. Ferdinand and Isabella were waiting just inside the door, outraged that she had spent the night away from home, and she gave them a particularly large breakfast as a form of

106

apology. She brought in the paper, then went upstairs to change. For some reason, instead of putting a load of clothes in the washer, going to the grocery store, and paying her bills, she felt like lying on her bed and daydreaming.

"It must be love," she told herself in the mirror, and started gathering up her laundry.

She thought of Jared that night in bed, and she thought of him while she was driving to work the next day. Every time the telephone rang, either at home or in her office, she found herself wondering if Jared was the caller. As days went by, she became worried and then a little angry that he didn't call. Last time he had waited until Thursday, but Thursday came and went without a word, and she began to face the possibility that she had seen Jared for the last time. By the time the telephone rang in her office on Saturday morning, she had decided that Jared was a heel, she was a fool, and having settled that, it was time to go on with her life.

When she heard Jared's voice, she felt furious. His explanation that he had been in Los Angeles and hadn't been able to pry her unlisted home telephone number out of the information operator did nothing to pacify her.

"My office number is listed, you know. You could have called me here," she said abruptly, remembering how scared and angry she'd felt when he hadn't called.

"Well, I knew I'd be back this morning, so I decided to wait." His voice grew a little quieter. "I can tell I made a mistake, so I apologize. Have you already made plans for this afternoon?"

Rebecca hesitated. There wasn't much point in being angry anymore now. He had called, if belatedly, and he did still want to see her. The problem was that she couldn't stop feeling hurt.

"From the silence that's fallen, I gather there's some question in your mind. One thing I'd like to say is that if you feel you'd like to slow things down, don't think I'll insist on making love again. I realize that we may have gotten a little ahead of ourselves last week."

Her anger dissolved. Jared was always so considerate of her feelings—except when it came to telephone calls, she reminded herself. But now she could accept that.

"I'd like to see you this afternoon," she said, her voice soft now instead of accusatory. "You said something about a hike."

"I thought we could drive up Mt. Tamalpais and hike down into Muir Woods, if you'd like. There should be plenty of wildflowers around, and it looks like a nice day."

"Do I need to wear boots?"

"Just walking shoes, but I assume you'll have to go home and change. Why don't I meet you there in about three hours with some sandwiches?"

Rebecca smiled so broadly she was sure he would hear it in her voice. "I can make that, I think. I just have two more appointments."

"Good." His voice deepened suddenly. "I'll be looking forward to it."

She was still smiling when she hung up. It promised to be a good day after all. Jared had called. Why had she been so quick to doubt him?

The rest of the morning went smoothly, and she arrived home with only a few minutes to change before Jared was due. After some thought she decided on her old beat-up loafers to walk in. They were ugly but comfortable, and he probably wouldn't be pleased if her feet started to hurt and she couldn't keep up. She had a pair of blue jeans that she'd worn just once. They were a little tight, but today that didn't seem as much of a drawback as it once had. Then she could wear a loose plaid cotton blouse and carry a sweater. It was usually chilly in Muir Woods, with the tall redwoods blocking most of the sun. Even on the warmest days it was pleasant there, and today was just a normal day for San Francisco—clear but windy and brisk. There was fog a little closer to the coast, but so far her neighborhood at least had escaped.

The phone rang as she was buttoning her blouse, and she hurried downstairs to let Jared through the gate. By the time she'd checked all her buttons and zippers, he was at the door, and when she opened it, he put a paper bag down carefully on the step and put his arms around her. His lips were warm and soft and his mustache seemed unusually prickly. She could smell the faint leathery scent that seemed to come from his shaving cream or soap, and her body molded itself to his as his hands moved down her back.

"Mmmm," he murmured as his hands traveled over the back of her jeans. "Are you sure you'll be able to walk in these?"

Rebecca pulled away. "Of course," she said with as much dignity as she could manage. "Don't you like them?"

"Like them? I love them." He backed away to get a better view. "Turn around."

She pivoted rather quickly, realizing that they were still in the open doorway. "Why don't you come in?"

"Good idea." He picked up the bag and carried it to the kitchen. "Since it's already past noon, we may want to eat here before we leave. But first I have a question." He sat down at the table, and Rebecca did the same. "Were you really mad at me for not calling you earlier?"

"Yes, I was," Rebecca said, determined not to apologize. He looked very charming somehow, in jeans

109

and a red flannel shirt with the sleeves rolled up above his elbows, and she was tempted to discount her earlier distress.

"Why? Did it get in the way of other plans you wanted to make?"

"No. But after the middle of the week, I began to wonder if you'd call at all. And that made me nervous and that made me angry."

He thought for a moment. "I'll try to do better, but for future reference, you can always call me. This week I wasn't at home anyway, but from now on, don't sit around wondering. If I say I'll call, I will, but if it's not soon enough for you, then you should call me." He smiled a little as if to soften his last words. "Okay?"

"Okay." She smiled back, feeling very happy to be with him. "Let's eat."

"Do you want the chopped chicken liver or the liverwurst sandwich?" Jared asked, busily extracting wrapped parcels from the bag.

She wrinkled her nose. "Neither."

"Good," he said, "because all I have are turkey and roast beef."

"Very funny."

She ate a turkey sandwich, looking at him across the table. She loved the shape of his forearms, the way his hair curled, his bristly mustache.

"You have a very nice smile," he said, and she realized that she had been smiling just from the pleasure of being with him, eating sandwiches and drinking root beer. He looked at her with such tenderness that her heart seemed to turn over, and she had to look away for a moment.

He drew an audible breath, and she looked back at him as he began to gather the paper wrappers and other remnants of their lunch. "If we're going to keep things cool, we'd better leave," he said, and she nodded. She wasn't at all sure she wanted to keep things cool, but it seemed best to acquiesce. Things between them seemed to develop nicely without any careful planning, and she was content at the prospect of being with him under whatever circumstances he chose.

They decided to take her car after Jared reluctantly admitted that the Volvo was somewhat averse to long climbs, so Rebecca drove across the Golden Gate Bridge and through Mill Valley to Mount Tamalpais. At times Jared's hand rested warmly on her knee, and she glanced at him as often as she dared, trying to absorb every nuance of his presence, to remember every detail of the day. After all, she wouldn't see him again for a week.

She pulled off the road near the start of the trail, parking carefully in the dirt near the edge of a sloping ridge. The hiking trail stood out brown and narrow as they looked across the meadow and down into the deep green expanse of the woods. They walked single file along the ridge, Jared in front, and Rebecca admired his slender thighs and narrow rear. Even the backs of his ears were dear to her, but she forced herself to admire her surroundings as well as her escort.

And it was a beautiful day and a wonderful time of year for the hike. Scarlet pimpernels and blue owl's clover crowded the track, while farther down in the meadow they could see golden poppies, the tiny flowers of blue-eyed grass, purple thistles, and blue lupine and larkspur. Pink and blue morning glories lined the ridges above the trail, opened to the sun, and bumblebees were busy everywhere, their legs obviously laden with pollen.

It was hot along the trail where they were fully exposed to the afternoon sun, and Rebecca had begun to regret her choice of clothes when the path twisted and

111

dropped into a cool, damp, wooded glen. Branches of silvery sage bushes met across the trail, releasing their fragrance as Jared and Rebecca pushed them aside.

"For once we're hidden from view," Jared said, turning and opening his arms. She stepped up to him as if she'd always belonged in his embrace, and the sage closed around them as their lips met.

Rebecca's response was immediate and violent, but she restrained it as best she could. That was neither the time nor the place to make love, despite the fact that her heart was pounding and her nipples were already hard against Jared's chest. As if in answer to her thought, his hands moved between their bodies, cupping each breast and stroking it with his thumb.

A small sound escaped from her throat and she backed away, but he leaned forward so that their lips still touched, and his hands never left her body, moving instead to her tightly encased thighs. The scent of sage filled her nostrils and she half fell against him, overwhelmed by desire.

"Not here," she gasped as his fingers stroked the inner seams of her jeans.

He wrapped his arms around her then and stroked her hair, his mustache tickling her temple as he spoke. "This was going to be just a preview of coming attractions, but somehow it got out of hand."

She nodded against his neck, enjoying the warmth of his skin on her cheek.

"Maybe this isn't the time to say so," he went on, "but I think if we saw each other a little more often— if we saw each other during the week to cook dinner together or to see a movie—we'd be less obsessed with sex. The way things are now, we could easily spend all our time together in bed."

"But that's just because it's all so new," she said, stepping back a little to look at him.

"Fine. Then when we're bored to death with each other, we can see each other less often." He smiled and clapped her on the shoulders, as if everything was settled, and she reached up absently to straighten a lock of his brown hair between her fingers.

It was nice that he wanted to see her more often, but it was dangerous too. She could easily imagine them being very close for several months and then Jared leaving, either because he was bored or because he was afraid to make a commitment. She didn't understand him very well yet, but she knew enough about herself to know that if she let things progress naturally, she'd be very much in love with Jared and very unwilling to let him go.

"What are you thinking?" he asked, and she smiled sadly into his gray eyes, sure that she could never tell him. He looked at her for a moment, then shrugged. "Then shall we hike on?" he asked, and she nodded.

"You go first for a while," he said. "I want to enjoy a rear view of you in those jeans."

So on they walked, down the meadow into the redwood forest, then along a dark, piny circular trail and back into the sun and up to her car. Rebecca's thoughts circled continuously along the way—should she live for the moment or protect herself from future pain? Should she go for broke or settle for a small, carefully measured portion of happiness? She drove home still wondering, and they were both silent in the car.

"Shall I come in?" Jared asked when she pulled into her garage, and she turned to him in surprise.

"Of course." He looked very serious, and she put her hand lightly on his arm. "I want to be with you."

"Good." He exhaled audibly and took her into his arms. "Then let's go in," he murmured, kissing her throat and the skin revealed by the V of her blouse.

She laughed softly. "Yes, let's. We didn't go through all that self-restraint to end up making love in bucket seats."

As if in a race, they went into the house and up the stairs to the bedroom. Rebecca threw back the covers and turned to find Jared already half undressed. With frantic fingers she unbuttoned her own blouse and tossed it on the chair. Then Jared was naked and came to help her with the rest of her clothes as she admired his body, seen for the first time in daylight.

He was tan except for the area that was usually covered by swimming trunks, and his body was slender without appearing weak. His shoulders were broad, his thighs long and taut with muscle, and his stomach was slightly concave. She could see the faint outline of his ribs, and she ran one finger tentatively down his side. He kneeled to pull her clothes over her feet and she cupped his head in her hands, then gripped his shoulders strongly as his hands slid up her thighs.

"Come to bed," she said huskily, and fell back on the rainbow-striped sheet.

He stood up, and her eyes were riveted on him as he stepped toward the bed. Just the sight of him aroused her to feverish urgency. She'd been waiting for him for hours, she realized as she put one hand on each side of his hips and pulled him over her. He bent to her breasts, then moved down the bed as his lips played over her stomach, but she drew him upward, her hips already twisting in anticipation.

"Now," she moaned, and he kissed her briefly before setting himself between her knees.

She guided him easily to the heart of her, half satisfied just to feel him there, and for a few moments she was at peace, smiling up at him as their bodies moved in gentle rhythm. Then an electric surge of pleasure caught her and she tossed her head on the pillow, her fingers digging urgently into his buttocks as her cries incited him. She seemed to ride an endless crest, mindlessly accepting the sensations that coursed through her body, helplessly relying on him to fulfill her needs.

She didn't know if hours or minutes passed before she became somewhat calmer and more aware of her surroundings. With a little effort she relaxed, realizing for the first time that their bodies were drenched in perspiration, that her nails were digging into Jared's skin, and that she had been embarrassingly noisy. She moved her hands up to caress his back, his hair, his face, and he kissed her, his tongue probing her mouth demandingly as his movements quickened. He groaned suddenly and she sighed, feeling a sudden warm balm that was infinitely soothing.

"I love you," she whispered too softly for him to hear. It was foolish, it was dangerous, and it was too early, but her decision was made. She would go for broke.

CHAPTER SEVEN

"I think you're right," she said later as they sat over dinner in a small Chinese restaurant. "We should see each other more often so we can be better friends." She stopped and took a large bite of fried prawn. The next move was up to him.

He seemed pleased, if not ecstatic. He was looking at her a little quizzically, and she smiled suddenly. His hair was a little damp from the shower, and he still had on his hiking clothes. She thought she'd never seen a more handsome man.

"In that case, I have two questions for you," he said.

"Yes?" He was smiling now, so everything must be all right.

"First, what are you doing tomorrow night, and second, what does the *D* stand for?"

Rebecca sighed. "Tomorrow night maybe we could do something together, if you like. As for the second question, I've never told anyone my first name since I was five or six. Why should I start now?"

He reached across the table for her hand. "So that we can be better friends."

She nodded, resigned. The more fuss she made about it, the harder it would be to tell him in the end. "The *D* is for Diamond."

"Diamond. I rather like it. Do you play golf?"

"No."

"Too bad. If you did you could be a diamond in the rough."

She had to laugh, but she didn't want him to misunderstand. "I'm very sensitive about my name. My mother named me after a poem she'd read, but the name was always too unusual for me, and by the time I'd started school I knew I wanted something different."

"So how does your mother feel about you using your middle name?"

"My mother died three years ago," Rebecca said softly. "I think she was sorry that I didn't like the name she gave me, but she understood my reasons, so it was never an issue between us."

Jared squeezed her hand. "I'm sure your parents were very proud of you."

"Yes." Rebecca smiled. "I'm the first in my family to go to college, so my father is quite in awe of me. And so was my mother, when she was alive. Once my brother gets his degree, some of the novelty should wear off."

"You see what a wonderful idea this was? I didn't even know you had a brother. You've been much too quiet about yourself."

Rebecca shrugged. "Yes, I have a brother, Richard, who's almost nineteen. And I have a new stepmother, whom I don't see very often. And that's about it, as far as my family goes."

Jared leaned back a little in his chair. "Well, I have one mother, one sister, and innumerable stepfathers. You already know quite a bit about my family."

"And how is your sister, while we're on the subject?"

Jared grimaced. "She looks into the mirror and says she's too fat. She looks just fine to me."

"Has she stopped gaining weight?" Rebecca asked, and he shook his head. "Then just relax and leave it up to Alice. These things take time, and I'm not sure they ever resolve themselves perfectly."

His shoulders slumped. "You mean this is a lifelong problem?"

"It may be," Rebecca said. "It's too soon to say."

"Then damn my mother and Meri's father," he said in a very quiet voice. "She's paying for their selfishness." The creases in his face deepened, and she looked with compassion at his sudden despair.

"Let's go home," she suggested quietly, putting her free hand on top of his, and he nodded to the waiter.

Home for that night meant her condominium. The following night it was Jared's house. Rebecca began carrying a change of clothes with her in the car, and as the days went by she more often asked Madeleine to feed her cats for her. By the end of the second week, they actually spent their first full night together without making love. Rebecca woke up in the morning with Jared curled up warm and sleeping against her back, and she laughed softly.

"I think there's something special about having slept together all night," she said in answer to his sleepy inquiry, "but when I think about it more my attitude seems a little silly. Why should this night mean more to me than any of the others?"

Jared gave a rumbling chuckle. "Now that you've said that, I hesitate to ruin such a perfect night. But I am feeling rather well rested, and I thought perhaps . . ." His hand moved suggestively over her naked breasts, and she snuggled up to him more closely.

"Can you see what time it is?" she asked. He lifted himself on one elbow and groaned.

"It's time for me to get up," he said. "The alarm clock should go off in exactly thirty seconds."

"Leaving all my illusions intact." She turned over to embrace him, tucking herself into the familiar contours of his body, and he kissed her.

"Diamond," he murmured. It had become his endearment to her, a name he only used privately, and she had begun to value it for that reason. He pushed the button on the alarm clock the instant the radio came on and jumped out of bed, leaving her a little forlorn. "If I'm going to make your eggs, I'd better get cracking," he said, and laughed.

Rebecca sighed dramatically. "I'd hoped you'd given up those terrible puns," she complained. "Have you no pride?"

"Very little," he said, and disappeared into the bathroom.

"Sometime I'd like you to meet my friends Cal and Madeleine," she told him over breakfast. "Madeleine's awfully pregnant now, so we might be better off waiting. The baby's due"—she thought for a minute—"next week."

Jared took several bites of toast. "I'm not really enamored of these happy family scenes, you know. Right now it's all bliss and crocheted booties, but in three years they'll be squabbling and the baby will have nervous tics, and in four years they'll be divorced and the kid will have its own psychiatrist."

Rebecca stared at him, astonished. "How can you say that?" She took a sip of coffee to calm down, and scalded her tongue. "Many families stay together quite happily."

Jared made a face. "I know. I shouldn't judge everyone by my own experience."

"That's true." Rebecca was glad to explain away his lapse in sensitivity. "You have a rather unusual family."

"I wasn't thinking of my family, actually." Jared looked at her very seriously, and she clenched her fingers nervously. "I was thinking of myself. One day I'm madly in love with a woman who is the most charming, beautiful, intelligent creature in the world. I'm on top of the world, and then the next day I've started to get used to her somehow, and I no longer appreciate her the way I once did. I think I'm like my mother—I'm prone to infatuation rather than love. I'm a walking example of someone who should never marry."

It was a searing pain, like a flame cutting through her chest, and she turned her face away. She didn't know him at all anymore; he was an unfeeling stranger. He was warning her off, that much was clear. Right from the beginning he'd said that marriage wasn't for him. She'd accepted that, or tried to, but this pronouncement that he would suddenly lose interest in her was harsher than she'd ever expected. She knew her expression was frozen as she turned back to her eggs. The last forkful was cold and flavorless, and it seemed to choke her as she swallowed.

"I don't really believe that about you," she said finally. "I don't believe it about our relationship." Her throat was very tight, and her voice sounded thin and high.

Jared shook his head. "I know you don't believe it, but I'm fickle and changeable, and I care about you too much right now not to prepare you for the end." His voice, too, seemed to be forced through a fine crack in his throat. "I'm not enjoying this, but I have to be as honest with you as I can."

She bit her lip. She'd decided to go for broke, and suddenly they seemed close to the end. "It doesn't feel to me as if I'm just a passing fancy. I've decided that the real thing exists, and I think this is it. And you want to throw it away?" She pushed her plate from her as if she were rejecting everything he had said, and then a further thought occurred to her. "Does this have anything to do with the fact that we didn't make love last night?"

Jared stood up and walked around the table to put his hands on her shoulders. "No. Not at all. And I'm not saying everything's over. I'm just reminding you that the end will come, that's all." He bent and kissed her in back of the ear, but she was unmoved. "And personally I hope the end is far away," he added, and she reached up to cover his hands with her own.

"I think I need some time to think this through," she said finally, and stood. "And we'd both better get to work."

The next day Madeleine's baby was born. Rebecca had told Jared she wanted some time alone, so she had plenty of time to shop. When Madeleine and the baby, Emily, had been home from the hospital for a few days, Rebecca called and then walked across the tiny lawn, carrying an armful of presents stacked up to her chin.

While Madeleine opened the packages, Rebecca watched the sleeping baby, fascinated by her tiny round mouth, her pink little fingers. She found herself listening attentively as Madeleine described feeding schedules and discussed the pros and cons of various kinds of diapers, topics that had always bored Rebecca in the past. Even more surprising, she wanted to hold Emily as soon as she woke up.

"I always thought you weren't very interested in children," Madeleine remarked as Rebecca rocked Emily while she sat in the new bentwood rocker.

Rebecca tried to analyze her feelings. It seemed to her that since she had met Jared, the idea of marriage and a family had begun to appeal to her. Until he'd indicated that his feelings for her were so temporary, she'd been very happy with him, more happy than she'd ever been before. And, of course, her thirtieth birthday was approaching. She no longer had the luxury of an infinite amount of time in which to change her mind about having children. She'd seen now what was possible for her, and she was beginning to want it all—her work, love, a husband, a baby.

None of those things would come from Jared, it seemed. But she was a determined woman, and she hadn't given up yet. As she rocked the baby, she tried to decide what to do.

Jared called two days later, plaintively wondering if she hadn't had enough time alone.

"I think so," she said, "but I can't come over tonight. I'm babysitting for Madeleine for two hours. Do you want to come up here?"

Jared sighed. "I suppose this means that I'll be forced to witness charming domestic scenes of you soothing a squalling infant, and so on."

Rebecca shrugged, no longer so enthusiastic about seeing him. "It's up to you," she said.

"Why don't I come up in a couple of hours. Then you'll be free when I get there. I know you're unhappy with me, and I think we should talk."

"Okay," she said. "If I'm not home, I'll be next door."

While the baby slept, she thought. Why was Jared so afraid of making a commitment? Why did he insist on such sarcasm about marriage and domesticity? Rebecca had never really desired marriage, not until now at least, but she'd never been cynical about it either. Of course her background was more stable than Jared's, more conducive to optimism about the permanency of human relationships.

She had a short, whispered conference with Madeleine after she and Cal returned from the movie, and Madeleine was firm. "If you love Jared and you think you'd be happy with him for the rest of your life, then you can feel that way about another man too. So if Jared's afraid of you, dump him and find someone else."

Rebecca nearly gasped. "I thought you were supposed to be a romantic, always telling people that Mr. Right would come along."

Madeleine wrinkled her nose. "I never said there was only one Mr. Right in the world for each woman, did I? Why, if there was only one, the odds against meeting him would be incredible."

"I suppose." Rebecca walked home slowly, a little disturbed by Madeleine's advice. Things didn't seem that bad to her, and she definitely didn't want to lose Jared. She had to give him time.

When he appeared at the door, she knew Madeleine was wrong. It was Jared she wanted, no one else, and she'd take him on any terms. His gray eyes were a little shadowed, his face somber, and she fell into his arms as if they'd been apart for weeks. His hands and mouth were warm and urgent, and she responded immediately.

"Do you want to talk?" Jared asked, and she nuzzled his neck.

"Come to bed," she said. "We can talk later."

They went upstairs hand in hand and undressed themselves rather quickly, then fell into bed and clung together with hungry desperation. They held each other for a moment, their lips joined in a tender kiss that spoke of their mutual need. Then Rebecca pushed him back on the bed, placing her hands on either side of his shoulders.

She adored his body, the muscles of his upper arms, the way his chest narrowed to his waist, the curve and tuck of his buttocks. And tonight she was going to find out all about him. She wanted to devote herself to a thorough appreciation of every part of him. This time her own sexual satisfaction was irrelevant, because she was going to satisfy her desire to know him more intimately than any woman ever had.

She kissed every inch of his face, her fingers stroking his hair as she discovered the textures of his skin—the corners of his eyes, his earlobes, his mustache, and his chin. She licked with her tongue, tasting his lips, his eyelids, and his ears. He reached up to pull her close but she resisted, stiffening her arms.

"Let me," she whispered, and he released her, looking at her with an unreadable question in his eyes. She moved her mouth over his neck, where the skin was warm and soft, and down to the curly hairs of his chest. She circled his nipples with her tongue, gratified by his low moans as she explored his responses. She caressed one tiny nipple with her fingers while her lips surrounded the other, and Jared's hands moved down her back, stroking her buttocks and the backs of her thighs.

She moved lower then, tantalizing him as she stroked and kissed his stomach and thighs. They were both breathing loudly, completely intent upon what she was doing, and their bodies were as warm as if they'd been lying in the sun. She was more excited than she'd ever been, feeling in control of herself and of Jared's reactions, a kind of power that she'd never experienced before.

When her teasing finally ended, his sharp inhalation was profoundly rewarding, and she caressed him eagerly with her lips and tongue and fingers. He pushed away abruptly only to pull her hips over his, and she joined with him easily, moving her hips slowly and deliciously.

"Diamond, my diamond," Jared murmured softly. Her climax was slow in coming and then seemed to extend indefinitely while she rode on him, her back arched so strongly that she saw only the ceiling when she opened her eyes. Hot tears ran down her cheeks as she felt him shudder, and they rolled to their sides and lay quietly together for several minutes while her tears rolled into the pillow.

His finger brushed her cheek then, and she knew he had noticed that she was crying. "Are you leaving me?" he asked, and she shook her head violently, afraid to trust her voice.

"Not until you want me to," she said. "I want us to have as much time together as we can."

"So do I," he whispered, pulling her close so that she could lie with her head on his shoulder.

"Well, let's make every minute count," Rebecca said. "We'll enjoy what we have for as long as we have it, and let the future take care of itself."

"Good idea." Jared pulled her still closer, then tucked the covers around both of them. "Shall we get some sleep?" he asked, and she murmured an assent. Tomorrow would be a much better day, she was sure.

"Let's have a big night out tomorrow and go to the opera," Jared suggested the next morning. "We can get all dressed up and have a nice dinner, the works."

Rebecca was delighted. "I've never even been to the opera," she told him, already imagining the new dress she would buy. "Are you sure you can get tickets this late?"

Jared grinned. "One way or another, I'll get some tickets. Will you come to my place tonight?"

Rebecca hesitated. "I'll have to do some shopping up here, so maybe I'd better not."

"I'll come here after work, then, if that's all right,"

he said, and she leaned across the table to kiss him on the cheek. He'd never seemed so loving, so openly wanting to be with her.

He doesn't trust himself, she thought, watching him happily as he loaded his dishes in the dishwasher. He was afraid of commitment, but in time he'd discover that their relationship was different from others he'd had. As they spent more and more time together, he'd see how good everything was, and he'd come to want permanency just the way she had.

She stood and put her arms around his waist, her breasts flattening against his back. "I have to go," she said, kissing him under his ear. "But I'll see you tonight."

"Buy a dress that matches your eyes," he said as she was closing the door, and several times on her way to work she lifted her face to the rearview mirror.

She'd never been particularly proud of her eyes, and she couldn't really imagine a hazel dress. Maybe brown with yellow flecks, she thought ridiculously as she went up in the elevator to her office. She was so happy even the oppressively bouncy music that was piped into the elevator didn't annoy her. Neither did the fact that her door stuck and she had to kick it open, nor the fact that her first patients were twenty minutes late.

Being in love was wonderful, she reflected as she ate a sandwich in the early afternoon. It made trivial problems seem even more trivial, it made sandwiches taste good, and it would even give her enough energy to go shopping tonight after her seven o'clock appointment.

As it happened, she had very little time to shop once she had driven back to the city, so she presented herself at the most expensive dress shop she knew of and asked for a dress that matched her eyes. The saleswoman was predictably surprised by her request, but disappeared into a back room and reappeared several minutes later with a raw silk dress the color of dark honey.

It was a dress and matching coat, actually, Rebecca saw, and she nearly ran out of the shop when she heard the price. But if there was ever a time to splurge on herself, this was it. And after she saw the way the coat buttoned diagonally up the front to a mandarin collar, she couldn't resist trying it on. It fit perfectly, and she only winced a little as she wrote out the check.

And it was all worth it the next night at the opera, where for the first time in her life she felt herself to be among the best-dressed women present. And it was worth it again two weeks later, when they went to the symphony and afterward to a late supper. All summer they were together more than they were apart, and by September Rebecca thought there was very little they hadn't done together.

They'd been to the beach and to the mountains, to a jazz concert and a mariachi band. They'd gone hiking, swimming, and sailing. And she had told Jared over and over that she loved him, and he had said nothing in return.

She didn't need marriage to be happy, she told herself every night as she fell asleep in his arms. And she didn't need a child, either. Still, the implication that the relationship was still temporary bothered her more and more. Her lovemaking grew tense and frantic, her conversations with Jared irritable. She began waking up at four o'clock in the morning and was unable to get back to sleep.

At work she felt uninspired, as if everything she did fell flat. The point was brought home to her strongly one evening when in a kind of escape from Jared, she bought Cal and Madeleine a Chinese dinner. Cal remarked, "Some of our colleagues are still telling that story about the time you walked out and left that family locked in your office."

"It wasn't really like that," Rebecca explained quickly to Madeleine. "They kept trying to lock their teenager in the house at night, and he kept escaping. So they just put on more and more locks and bolts and bars. So one day in my office I told them I was going to get a drink of water and I locked the door very noisily behind me."

Madeleine frowned.

"Well, I stood right outside the door so I could let them out instantly, but of course they started plotting their escape and their son managed to open the door with his father's credit card."

"And so?" Madeleine asked, still looking quite disapproving.

"They understood much better how they were challenging their son, and they appreciated him more, too. It was a big breakthrough—it really was," she insisted as Madeleine continued to look skeptical. "And it also taught me that I needed much better locks on my door."

"I think it's a perfect example of family therapy," Cal said, "but by now that story has been overused. So give me some new ones to tell."

Rebecca thought for a while. That incident had occurred early in the summer, when she'd been in love and exhilarated. During that time she'd been right on top of her job, and she'd been more daring than usual. Being around Jared had made her a little less prim and more willing to try new tactics. He'd been good for her back then.

"I haven't done anything of interest lately," she told Cal. "Now that I think of it, I probably haven't been earning my fee."

"Nonsense," he said, but she wasn't so sure. She was just dragging through the days, tired and strained, because she was trying to resign herself to an unsatisfactory situation. She'd have to take some steps to help herself.

"I need a commitment from you," she told Jared the next night. "Something I can hold on to."

"I didn't think you were interested in marriage," he said, looking cornered.

"I didn't say marriage, although I'd like that to be a possibility," Rebecca said. "It's not marriage I want, it's you—your love, your willingness to stick by our relationship even during the times it's not perfect."

He shook his head, and she felt a sinking sensation in her stomach. "I can't promise you that—it wouldn't be fair."

"Do you need more time?" she asked.

He shook his head again. "Time isn't the problem. I just don't want to make a promise I might not keep."

"So what shall we do," she asked, her voice thick with tears. "Is this the end?"

He looked away for a moment, either to hide his feelings or because he couldn't bear to see hers. "You'll have to decide," he said softly. "It's you who want more."

She hesitated for a moment, wondering if she could stand to say she wouldn't see him again, if she could let him go. "Can't you change your mind? Can't you try?" she asked.

"No," he said. "I can't." And the flatness of his reply gave her the courage she needed.

"Then this is it." She ducked her head to hide the sudden tears, and when he brushed her cheek with his fingertips a loud sob escaped from her throat. "I just can't go on with you like this," she said. "It's hurting me too much."

"I know." He leaned forward to kiss her cheek, and she fell into his arms.

"Just hold me for a few minutes," she whispered.

"For as long as you want," was his reply, and she asked herself bitterly if that wasn't the closest he'd ever come to making a commitment to her.

She stayed close to him for several minutes, listening to the familiar thump of his heart, breathing the clean smell of his shirt. Then, her throat so tight she could hardly breathe, she stood up to leave.

"If you want to call me, anytime at all, I'll be here," Jared said. It almost sounded like a commitment again, but it wasn't enough to change her mind.

"We need some time apart, at least," she said at the door. "And I'm talking about months, not days. But maybe sometime . . ."

She turned suddenly and left. She'd closed the door behind her, but when she got in the car she saw that Jared was standing on the step, his hands in his pockets. His eyes seemed large and dark with pain, and his mouth was drawn down in a thin line. Under the porch light the creases that ran between his nose and the corners of his mouth seemed deeper, but all that was only a trick of the light. He'd had every opportunity to keep her, she reminded herself as she started her car. If his feelings were as uncertain as he said, he shouldn't be feeling hurt now. It was just an earlier end to their affair than he'd planned.

She drove home carefully, forcing herself to concentrate and refusing to shed a single tear. Once she was safe in her own house, then she could let the barriers down. She parked in her garage and went into the kitchen, breaking into a run as she heard the phone begin to ring.

130

"Hello?" she gasped, wishing unreasonably that it would be Jared.

"It's me," he said, and she leaned against the counter, limp with relief. He'd realized how much he loved her, and now everything would be all right.

"I was worried about you driving home when you were upset. I just wanted to make sure that you were all right."

"I'm fine." She choked on the words and swallowed hard while she waited to see if anything else would follow. There was a silence, and she realized they had nothing more to say to each other. " 'Bye," she said, and dropped the receiver into its cradle. She'd held herself in check as long as she could.

She ran blindly upstairs, obeying some impulse from long ago to retreat into her bedroom and hide her grief from the world. And she cried. Wildly and horribly she sobbed and gasped until her eyes were swollen almost shut and her throat felt as if it had been rubbed with an emery board. And even then it wasn't finished. The tears continued to streak her cheeks long after she would have thought she'd cried out every ounce of fluid in her body. They fell into the cats' dinners, into the bowl of tomato soup she'd fixed herself, and into her toothbrush before she went to bed.

She went to work the next morning with her eyes red and swollen even after the application of ice packs. This was what she'd dreaded all along—the depression, the inability to focus on her patients that she'd known would come at the end of the affair. She was surprised to find that nothing was as terrible as she'd expected. Her patients were a welcome relief from her own unhappy thoughts, and she listened intently to their problems, grateful to forget her own for a while.

When she was alone, she felt terrible. Her chest hurt, her throat ached, her legs didn't want to move.

So after a few days she began calling friends, people she hadn't seen once she'd started spending so much time with Jared. She met people for dinner, for swimming, and to go to the movies. And finally, with some trepidation, she arranged to have lunch with Alice Fairweather, knowing that the topic of Jared's sister was almost certain to arise.

Rebecca and Alice met in a small pie and bread shop on Union Street, a place that served light dinners, where women could comfortably eat alone or in pairs. Over her cream of asparagus soup, Rebecca mentioned that she had been seeing Jared but had stopped.

"He's quite an attractive man," Alice said, stirring her own soup. "Too bad things didn't work out." Her brown eyes were sympathetic, but Rebecca was glad she'd disposed of the topic quickly. It was ridiculous to be jealous, but Jared had found Alice's curly red hair and trim figure appealing, and apparently the attraction was mutual.

"How's Meredith doing?" she asked.

"Well, she's keeping her weight up, but it's still a struggle. She's speaking up more in the group, though, and I think she'll do well if she sticks with it."

Rebecca nodded. "That's good."

"It's too bad she doesn't have a more normal family to depend on. Her brother seems to be the only person who really cares about her for her own sake. I can't tell if her mother and stepfather care about anyone or anything except keeping up appearances, and I certainly haven't been able to make them understand how serious Meredith's problem could be."

Rebecca murmured a reply, her mind on Jared. If his family was really so unloving, it made his feelings about marriage and commitment easier to understand. He'd never had firsthand experience of a happy family,

132

and now he was afraid that Meredith would be destroyed by her parents' inadequacies.

Alice turned to study the pies in the glass counter for a few seconds, then looked at Rebecca. "If you're feeling at loose ends, you might like to come with me to my cabin for the week of Columbus Day. It'll be a back-to-nature experience—kind of a chance to get away from it all for a while."

It sounded ideal. A break from her routine, leaving everything that reminded her of Jared, would surely do her good. And she had a few weeks left to reschedule her patients and prepare them for the interruption. As she and Alice began making lists of things to bring, she felt her spirits rise a little.

Early in the morning about three weeks later they stuffed the last bag of groceries into Alice's station wagon, and Rebecca locked her front door. It promised to be warm in San Luis Obispo County but it was still chilly in San Francisco, and she shivered a little in her thin blue cotton slacks and gauzy white top. Her sweater was buried somewhere in the back of the wagon, probably under a bag of charcoal, and she couldn't face trying to dig it out. She waved good-bye to Madeleine, who had come to her living room window, and climbed into the passenger seat. They were off.

It was several hours of driving and a rather boring trip once they had crossed the Santa Cruz Mountains. The nearly treeless hills were still dry and brown from the scorching summer sun, and they seemed to roll endlessly past her window. She and Alice chatted desultorily for a while and then fell silent, and Rebecca tried not to think about Jared. In February or March, if she still missed him, she'd call him. Of course, by then he'd be involved with someone else. But in the meantime she'd try to forget his serious gray eyes, his awful jokes, his firm, muscular body. She'd hope, somewhere in the back of her mind, that somehow he'd grow more willing to commit himself, or that she'd grow to want that less from him.

They turned onto a broad dirt road, and the dust that rose from the tires obscured her view. They passed an ancient Ford pickup truck turning into the dirt parking lot of a tiny, mustard-yellow grocery store, and Rebecca sat up. "We must be getting close."

Alice laughed. "Not really. There's a larger store farther up, near Christmas Cove, and my cabin is about six miles from that. I'm just taking you along the back roads."

Three deer jumped across the road in front of them, and Rebecca laughed. Soon they began seeing more squirrels and birds in the road, and then they were on a paved highway again for several thousand feet.

"Now we're close." Alice jumped out and unlocked a padlock to swing open a clumsy wooden gate that stretched across the road. "Just through the trees and around the bend."

"There's our water tank." She pointed to a small redwood tank that sat on top of a rise. It wasn't much bigger than her bathtub, Rebecca thought, wondering if she'd be able to shower.

Alice jumped out of the car again to unfasten some strands of barbed wire. That done, she drove up a faint track toward a small, weathered cabin that sat in the shade of two huge oak trees. Rebecca climbed out of the car as soon as it stopped and stretched gratefully. It was hot and still, and she could look back and see the dust their passage had raised.

The cabin had a long front porch, and Rebecca stood there and peered through the windows as Alice unlocked the door. They stepped right into the kitchen, and Alice inspected the top of the kitchen table, which stood just inside the door.

"Haven't had too many mice in here," she announced, and Rebecca looked around a little more closely. In the far corner of the kitchen was an old green sofa. Rebecca sat on it for a moment, finding it surprisingly comfortable, then went down a short hallway to discover a tiny bathroom and the bedroom.

"I'll hook up the gas and water," Alice said, producing a large white propane can.

"I'll unload the car and make some sandwiches," Rebecca offered, and began making trips back and forth to the car. She watched out of the corner of her eye as Alice lit a pilot light under the refrigerator and turned it on.

"I had a generator up here at one point," Alice said, "but I decided it was too noisy. The whole point of being here is to have quiet. So I ripped out all the wiring and went back to the original gas appliances. There!" She turned on the water at the sink, and a fairly healthy stream came out. "We'll have to be a little bit careful with the water, but we have enough for showers and the essentials," she reassured her friend.

She sat down at the kitchen table as Rebecca put out ham sandwiches and glasses of root beer. "After we eat, let's put our suits on and walk down to the lake. It's so hot, a swim will be nice."

Within the hour they were on their way to the lake, carrying towels, cooler, air mattress, and sun lotion. They had put jeans on over their bathing suits to protect their legs from the various thistles and stickers that grew beside and over the road, and Rebecca was secretly glad no one could see them as they trudged along. It was a bit of a scramble down to the water, but once they were on the shore it was pleasantly cool and breezy.

"This is actually a man-made reservoir," Alice said as she spread her towel across a patch of pine needles. "You can still see some of the trees that were growing in the area they flooded here."

Rebecca slipped off her jeans and put a tentative foot in the water. Like all such lakes, its bottom was muddy rather than sandy. Feeling glad that she had brought her old black bathing suit, which she didn't have to worry about ruining, she paddled and floated in the water until she felt cooled off, then struck out toward the center of the lake, away from the small inlet where Alice appeared to be napping.

By the time she swam back Alice had moved her towel to a sunnier spot and was coating herself with sun lotion. Rebecca stood on the shore and dripped for a few minutes, watching a woodpecker at work across the water, and then she saw with some dismay that a canoe was entering their inlet. She had been enjoying the quiet, and the boat was an intrusion into the isolation that she needed so badly. With any luck the man in the canoe would just paddle away again without landing or trying to strike up a conversation.

His face was turned away from them as he approached, so he might not even know they were there. Rebecca watched him more intently as he drew closer. There was something familiar about the curl of his hair and the way his shoulders stretched his shirt each time his paddles hit the water. In fact, she recognized the brown-and-white-striped shirt.

It had to be Jared! She looked around, trying to decide if she could disappear into the bushes, and then she shrugged, running her fingers through her tangled wet hair. They were adults, and if he stopped and recognized her, they'd just have to be cordial. Alice was sitting up, frowning sympathetically, and Rebecca was suddenly grateful for her presence as insurance that Rebecca and Jared could act like distant friends.

His boat was on the shore and he was stepping out, pulling it farther out of the water. "Hello, Rebecca, Alice." He nodded at each of them, watching them carefully, and as Rebecca replied, her eyes studied him hungrily. How were they going to manage even an inane conversation? There was either a lot to say, or there was nothing. He looked the same as ever, a little darker from the sun perhaps, and somehow a little more tired. She couldn't look at him without remembering everything that had happened between them. She imagined his fingers stroking her hair, his lips brushing her cheek, and she clenched her fingers tightly, hoping her face wasn't revealing her pain.

Jared and Alice were speculating on whether the coming winter would be wet or dry, and Rebecca tried to pay attention.

"You know," Alice was saying, "I just realized I forgot to bring flashlight batteries, and I want to get to the store before it closes. So Jared, if you'll keep Rebecca company and help her carry all these things back to the cabin, I'll just run back to the car and go."

It would have been awkward and embarrassing to protest, so Rebecca just stood there and watched Alice step into her jeans and climb up to the road. Alice probably meant well, thinking they could patch things up, but the separation between Rebecca and Jared was more than just a foolish quarrel. There were basic differences between them that they hadn't been able to reconcile, and this unexpected meeting didn't change anything. It just made life a little harder to bear.

"Diamond," Jared said as soon as Alice was out of sight, and somehow Rebecca was in his arms, her wet bathing suit pressed against his clothes. It felt wonderful to be in his embrace again, to feel his mustache against her cheek. She put her arms around him, pulling him against her as tightly as she could. Her fingers remembered the ridged contours of his back, the soft curl of his hair. Her hips remembered the pressure of his pelvis, his swelling desire.

"Kiss me," he murmured, and she turned her face toward him, feeling her lips begin to tremble. It was difficult, being with him like this and knowing they'd have to part again, but she was too weak to pull away. She needed the soft pressure of his lips on hers. How desperately she had missed his gentle, searching kisses. She was only human, and it would have taken a superhuman effort to resist him.

They stood there for long minutes, swaying together under the force of their desire, until Jared said, "We'd better hide the canoe and get these things back to the cabin before Alice gets back."

"Mmm," Rebecca agreed, and didn't move.

"I think we'd better do it now," Jared said a few minutes later, "before I abduct you and take you to my place in the canoe."

Rebecca still didn't move. "Alice would wonder what had happened to me."

"Alice would be able to guess," Jared said, and planted a row of kisses down the side of her neck. "But let's go to the cabin anyway. Then maybe we'll have time to talk privately."

Talk was the last thing she wanted, but she moved away slowly and began putting empty soda cans back in the cooler. Once they reached the cabin, she'd see to it that Jared had other things on his mind than conversation. She knew that talk would inevitably lead to disagreement, and she couldn't face losing him again so quickly.

CHAPTER EIGHT

Back at Alice's cabin, they headed instinctively for the green sofa and sat down. Rebecca turned to him, hooking her hand on the inside of his knee, and kissed him lightly. The tip of her tongue teased his lips for an instant, then withdrew. "Mmm," she said, feeling very much in control of the situation. "How long do you think Alice will be gone?"

"Not nearly long enough." His hands moved over the top of her bathing suit. "But I think we'll hear the car when it pulls up." He lifted one of the black straps over her shoulder and down past her elbow, carefully exposing one round white breast.

She groaned and pressed his lips more firmly as his fingers began to stroke her breast, cupping and circling without ever touching her tingling nipple. Her hand moved up his blue-jeaned thigh, her thumb rubbing hard against the seams as she felt him shift forward.

"Lie back." He pushed her gently until her head was resting against the arm of the sofa, then suddenly his mouth covered her nipple, warm and infinitely exciting. His lips squeezed her, his tongue circled softly, and his teeth nipped delicately until she could no longer stand it. Her hips writhed, encased in the swimming suit and blue jeans. His hand was warm against her stomach, but too far from her skin, separated by too many layers of thick fabric.

"There is a bedroom here," she said, and he shook his head against her breast.

"Maybe you can come to my place later tonight, or in the morning," he suggested, his moving lips and tongue spreading delightful sensations as he spoke.

"I don't want to be rude to Alice," she said, then sighed as his fingers explored the inner seams of her jeans. "She is my hostess, after all."

"I don't want to be frustrated," he countered, pulling on the other strap of her bathing suit. "I've been without you too long."

He covered one breast with his palm and rotated it softly while his tongue caressed the other nipple. "I remember all the textures of your body," he said, and Rebecca sat up suddenly.

"That's the car!"

Hurriedly she pulled up her suit and stood awkwardly in the middle of the room as Alice came noisily up the wooden steps and opened the front door.

"Was I gone too long?" Alice asked, standing in the doorway and surveying the cabin. Her right eye seemed to wink at Rebecca.

"I'm afraid we have a problem," she went on, as she came into the kitchen. "There was a message for me at the store from San Diego. My mother's ill, and I really should head south right away."

"Oh dear." Rebecca combed her hair with her fingers, trying to think logically. "How long would you stay down there?"

Alice frowned. "At least a week. And I hate to take the time to drive you home first, because that would delay me until morning. So I wondered if you could possibly . . ."

"I'll see that Rebecca gets home." Jared's voice made Rebecca jump. "Don't worry about a thing."

"Will that be all right?" Alice pressed her temples distractedly, and Rebecca hurried to reassure her.

"Let's get your things together so you can get started," Rebecca said, and the two of them went into the bedroom, where Alice had left her suitcase and sleeping bag. "I hope your mother will be okay," Rebecca said as they rolled up the sleeping bag, and was horrified when Alice snickered.

"Don't worry about my mother," Alice said as Rebecca stared at her. "She's fine. Just take advantage of this opportunity to straighten things out with Jared."

Rebecca thoughtfully picked up the battered leather suitcase. "What about your vacation?"

"I expect to have a lot of fun in San Diego. But if I'm going to get there at a reasonable hour, I'd better get going."

"Thanks, Alice," Rebecca whispered, and walked her to the car.

"Do you know," she said to Jared as Alice drove off, "her mother's not sick at all."

"Good." Jared put his arm around her and pulled her closer to his side. "I'd hate to profit by someone else's misfortune."

"But she's completely rearranged her whole vacation." Rebecca was beginning to feel guilty. She shouldn't have stood there so stupidly and let Alice go.

"And she wouldn't want her generosity to be wasted, would she?" He pulled her back up the steps and into the cabin, and locked the door firmly behind them.

"Now, where were we?"

She looked into the gray of his eyes, almost dizzy at the thought of what was to come, and he leaned forward and kissed her lightly on the nose.

"Let's make you a little more comfortable." He un-

141

buttoned the waist of her jeans and pulled the zipper tab down, watching her face as he kneeled in front of her to slide the denim down her legs. "Shoes, too," he said, untying them quickly, and then she was in her bathing suit.

He kissed her thighs, stroking the soft flesh as her heart began to race and she felt herself melting for him. She stroked his head, lifting the curls of his hair and letting them slide through her fingers. Their breathing sounded harsh in the silence of the cabin. Jared's fingers slid under the taut edges of her bathing suit, his teeth nipped at her inner thigh, and she gasped and pulled at his shoulders.

He stood, sliding his hands up her sides, and slipped off the straps of her suit to kiss each bare shoulder. Slowly he pulled the fabric down, baring her swollen breasts, her gently rounded stomach, until he kneeled in front of her again. His lips moved across her lower stomach, his mustache softly brushing her skin, but she pulled him to a standing position again and began unbuttoning his shirt. His fingers were at her breasts as she dropped his shirt on the floor and began unbuckling his belt.

"There!" she said softly as he finally stood naked in front of her, and emotion swelled in her chest as he kissed her and tenderly stroked her hair. She moved toward the sofa, drawing him along with her, and they lay down together, their lips always touching.

"I love you, Diamond," Jared said, his voice very deep, and she opened herself to him, almost bursting with joy.

They made love very slowly, constantly looking into each other's eyes, and she felt that he had finally realized the depth of their feelings for each other. How else could two people be so tender, so generous, and so exciting together? She had never even imagined anything like the soft, endless swell of sensation that began very subtly as his tongue found her breast and ended many minutes later with her sobbing his name.

They were very sweaty and very content as they lay together, and as she stroked his eyebrows with a delicate finger Rebecca promised herself that she would do nothing to spoil this interlude. He had told her he loved her. Admittedly he had been in the grip of sexual passion, but it was more than he'd ever offered her before. She would try to make it be enough.

They took a shower together in the tiny stall, turning off the water while they soaped each other thoroughly, and after they had rinsed off and dried, Rebecca slipped into an orange sundress.

"I don't have any clothes here," Jared remarked as he pulled up his jeans. "Which brings me to the question—should we stay here or canoe back to my family's place?"

Rebecca shrugged. "Whichever you prefer. You're the only one who's seen both places."

Jared thought for a moment. "Let's stay here. It's more primitive, and that makes it more special, somehow. As if we're cut off from the world, and nothing else matters."

"Fine." Her eyes burned for a moment and she looked away. She knew he was saying that here they could pretend for a few days without being reminded of the reality of their differences. They could pretend that this could go on forever, instead of ending in a week. "If you want to get your things, I'll see about starting some charcoal in the barbecue pit and learning my way around the kitchen."

They walked out together, and Rebecca pointed to a triangular device that sat on the stove. "What do you suppose that is?"

Jared laughed. "It's an old toaster. You put one slice

143

of bread in each side, light the burner, and there you are."

Rebecca studied it suspiciously. "Well, you can make the toast tomorrow, and we'll see if you're right."

"Trust me." He kissed her firmly. "I'll be back as soon as I can."

She found the bag of charcoal and carried it down the steps in time to see Jared jogging back toward the lake. She stood and watched him for a minute, admiring his even pace and his long stride. She would make this week a memorable one, she promised herself, since it was likely to be the last one they would have together. She set out a bucket of water and made a fire inside the circle of stones near the porch, then sat on the bottom step, her arms wrapped around her bent legs, and waited for Jared to come back.

He came back in his car, which surprised her for an instant, and they quickly unloaded his things. "I was originally supposed to be back at work on Tuesday," he said, "but I've arranged to spend the rest of the week down here with you."

"Good." She hugged him tightly in a rush of happiness. It had never even occurred to her that he might not be here for the full week, and she certainly wouldn't have been prepared to drive back Monday night.

She couldn't get enough of him. Quickly she remembered the special touches, the delicate strokes of her fingers and tongue that were certain to arouse him. She wanted to be part of him every minute, to feel him straining against her and to read the need in his darkening eyes. Her body seemed to acquire a new sensitivity along with her increased knowledge of him, so that each time their arms or hips brushed, each time Jared smiled at her, she could feel herself preparing for love.

144

After dinner they laid out their sleeping bags on the long wooden porch and made love twice to the night sounds of the owls and crickets. Sunday they made love when they woke up, ate breakfast and made love, went swimming and made love, drove the Volvo up into the hills and made love again under a stand of oaks. Three deer passed, their noses twitching delicately, and Rebecca nestled more closely into Jared's shoulder.

"I can't keep this up, you know," he told her, kissing the top of her head. "Not for more than a few days, anyway."

"I brought vitamins with me." She propped herself on one elbow and smiled down at him. "And anyway, what else is there to do out here in the country?"

He began ticking off possibilities on his fingers. "We could go boating or waterskiing on the lake, we could drive over to Hearst Castle and take a tour, we could drive down the coast to Solvang and eat Danish pastry, we can hike in the hills. . . ."

Rebecca pouted. "And you prefer all that to me?"

"You," he said, tapping her on the nose, "are the diamond in the crown of available activities."

"Here I am, lying naked in a nest of extremely prickly dried grass, and you make fun of my name." She sat up and began brushing herself off. "I may not give you any vitamins after all."

He pulled her down to kiss him. "I love you," he said, and she felt herself glowing. He was changing, moving toward a commitment. It was only a matter of time. If she could just be patient, he would come around.

"For a moment there I had delusions of making love again," Jared said, "but frankly I think it's a lost cause."

Rebecca nuzzled his neck. "Well, at least we made

up for lost time. I thought about this a lot while we were apart, and I really missed it."

"I missed you too." He kissed her, and she returned his kiss a little distractedly. There had been some constraint in their last remarks. Whether she had felt some tension in his body or heard it in his voice she didn't know. And she couldn't be sure what the problem was. Maybe she shouldn't have mentioned their separation and destroyed the pretense that everything had always been fine between them.

She sighed and sat up again, kissing his chest on her way. "Is there a handy stream to wash off in?"

Jared laughed. "The best I can offer is to pour a bottle of chilled mineral water over you."

Shuddering, she consented. "Just get it over with quickly," she begged as he took a bottle out of the cooler and began shaking it. The soda water felt like needles of ice as it sprayed her, and she dried shivering in the sunlight.

Jared seemed inordinately amused by the whole thing. "Do you really think that accomplished anything?" he asked as she slipped into her beige cotton slacks.

She nodded vigorously. "Absolutely. You probably wish I'd do the same for you."

"Some other time, maybe." Before she knew it, he was behind the wheel of the car. "Let's get back and whip up some dinner. All this exercise has left me with an enormous appetite."

"Well, we do need to keep your strength up," Rebecca said sweetly, resting her hand high on his thigh.

He turned and looked at her with a tender expression she'd never seen before. "Have I told you how much I love your voice?"

She shook her head, and he went on, "It's so nice and husky, it seems to flow into my ears, and it's never too loud or too shrill. I could listen to you talk for hours. And when you laugh, it's just delightful."

It was an emotional moment for her, and she hardly knew how to respond. He seemed to be opening up to her at last, appreciating her in ways she'd never hoped for, and she felt as if she would choke with gratitude and love.

"Thank you," she said finally, and he took her hand for a moment before he started the car.

The days seemed to blur in a haze of tangled, sun-browned arms and legs, elaborate preparation of meals on the ancient stove, soft laughter and tender whispers. There were occasional special events that punctuated the week and kept their time together from passing too slowly. On Friday Jared rented a speedboat and waterskis and undertook Rebecca's instruction in the art of staying upright in the water.

"I had no idea you were so stubborn," he told her after her tenth effort finally culminated in a three-minute run.

Rebecca shook her wet hair out of her face and laughed. "I thought you were going to say you had no idea I was so clumsy."

He looked noncommittal. "Want to try again?"

"Just one more time," she decided. "Just to prove I can really do it."

Afterward he eyed her speculatively until she began to fidget with the straps of her swimsuit.

"What is it?" she asked. "Are there bugs crawling on me or is my suit ripped?"

"I was just wondering if you ever give up."

Rebecca thought for a moment, twisting a damp strand of hair between her fingers. "I prefer not to."

"Now that I see how determined you can be, I have to wonder if you're determined to change me." His eyes met hers directly, and she felt a sudden constriction in her chest. This was it. They were about to have a disastrously serious conversation, and unless she was very careful, everything would fall apart again.

"I'm not trying to change you," she said, picking her words carefully. "I'm just trying to take things as they come."

They were sitting in the Volvo, the sun beating in on them through the windshield, and she felt as if she couldn't catch her breath.

"But surely your business is changing people."

"No." She shook her head. "People come to me because they want to change, and I help them. But I don't do it; they do."

"I haven't really changed, you know." His voice was so soft she had to lean forward to hear him. "When I saw you there at the lake, I realized how much you mean to me. Right now I love being with you, I enjoy everything about you. But I can't speak for tomorrow or the next day, much less six years from now. And if you're honest, you'll admit that you can't either." He frowned, almost as if something were hurting him, and Rebecca had to restrain herself from leaning over and kissing him. He looked very worried and very vulnerable, but this was hardly the time to offer sympathy.

"There's a leap of faith you have to make, a willingness to take a chance and invest everything you have in the relationship."

He shrugged. "That's fine in the beginning, but when the thrill begins to wear off, there's really nothing to prevent a divorce. And there shouldn't be, either. Once it's over, it's over."

"If there were children. . . ." Rebecca suggested, and he turned the key savagely in the ignition.

"If there were children, they'd suffer, the way Meredith has suffered."

"And did you suffer too?" she asked.

"Don't psychoanalyze me!" He threw the car into reverse and drove rather roughly back to the cabin, while Rebecca sat subdued beside him.

Their discussion certainly hadn't cleared the air, she thought as she unlocked the cabin door. And she had little incentive to try to talk further. A little hesitantly she went and sat down on the sofa. The idea of going into the bedroom with Jared and changing out of her swimsuit had very little appeal while there was tension between them. She didn't want to be naked and vulnerable unless they could be on better terms.

Jared came out of the bedroom in a pair of khaki shorts and a pale blue knit top. He stood at the refrigerator for a minute, looking over at her, and she sensed that he also wanted to put things right between them. Of course he wouldn't change his position, or she hers, but at least they could try to enjoy their last few days together.

"Come sit next to me," she said, and tried to smile. "It's no good our moping around and feeling miserable."

He sat down and draped one arm tentatively across her shoulders.

"We always seem to come up against the same barrier," he said, untangling her hair with gentle fingers. "And I'm not sure I understand why. We both know we have something very special. Do you think I'm denying that?"

Rebecca sighed. "In a way you are, by insisting it can't last."

"Let's just say I'm afraid it won't." He cupped her chin with his hands. "I want you with me every day for the foreseeable future. If you'd like to move into my place with me, I'd love to have you there. Is that the kind of commitment you need?"

She looked at him, at the gentleness in his eyes, and she hardly knew what to say. He was trying to give her what she needed. The problem was, the longer she knew him, the more she wanted from him. And it was time to be honest about that. She pulled his hands away from her face and held them tightly against her knees.

"The thing is, I want to have a baby."

Jared made a sound that was almost a laugh. "You want a baby? A few months ago you didn't even want to get married."

"My thirtieth birthday is coming up." She could hardly meet his eyes, she was so afraid of his reaction. "Somehow in reviewing my life, I've realized that now I want the whole thing. I want my profession, but I also want a husband, a fenced-in backyard, two children, and a dog." She hadn't explained it correctly, either. It wasn't any husband and children she wanted. It was Jared, and Jared's children.

"This is quite a surprise," he was saying. "I guess our goals are not as compatible as I thought they were."

Rebecca's heart gave a sickening thump. She could hear what he was leading up to, and she wasn't prepared to let him go. Not just when he was beginning to appreciate what they had together. She put her fingers over his lips.

"Let's just let things be while we're here," she said. "After all, we're on vacation."

After a moment he shrugged. "Why not?"

She rested her head on his shoulder, grateful for the warmth of his arm around her. She would close her mind to everything but the present and the immediate future. "Shall we take a tour of Hearst Castle tomorrow?" she asked, and he nodded.

"Why not?" he said again, and looked at her a little sadly, she thought. "If that's what you want."

She had wanted to see the castle, which had been constructed at great effort and expense with materials imported from Europe and decorated with William Randolph Hearst's collection of art and antiques. But somehow during the two-hour tour she found herself watching Jared instead of the rooms and gardens the guide was pointing out. Jared seemed tense and unhappy, and she also had the impression that something was worrying him. She herself was desperately trying to forget their conversation of the day before. Even more difficult was blocking out her memories of how unhappy she'd been several months back, before they had separated. If she was going to allow herself to feel that way again, she might as well say good-bye to Jared immediately.

She didn't know if she could find a way to make things work between them, but she was determined to make the next twenty-four hours good ones if she could. Despite her best efforts, though, she wasn't the cheerful, sunshiny companion she wanted to be. And Jared was too preoccupied to appreciate the occasional efforts she made. They rode the castle bus back down the hill to Jared's car, with Rebecca very much aware that a storm was brewing.

They stopped for a sandwich before they drove in silence back to the cabin.

"Would you like to take a walk?" Rebecca suggested. Walking always helped her think things out, and it seemed to calm her when she was upset.

Jared agreed without any apparent enthusiasm, and they changed quickly into jeans and heavy shoes, avoiding each other's eyes. They set out at a brisk pace on a dirt track that led up to a working cattle ranch, and for a time the only sounds were their steady footsteps and the occasional cry of a bird. A hawk circled overhead, and Jared touched Rebecca's arm to attract her attention to it.

They watched the hawk together for a moment, then lost sight of it when it dropped, apparently having sighted prey. Rebecca slipped her hand into Jared's and they walked on and on, higher into the hills. It was warm, and after about two hours they stopped to share a drink from Jared's canteen.

Being together with Jared, holding his hand, somehow made their problems seem minimal, although they hadn't talked about them this time. She'd never known such comfort with another person, such satisfaction in silent companionship, and she knew that she would fight to keep as much of him as she could. She would fight herself, her own desire for security, and she would win.

"I feel better now," she said, watching his unsmiling face. "How about you?"

"Yup," he said and grinned. "Me, too. I suppose that means we should head back, before we wear ourselves out completely."

She leaned over and kissed him on the cheek, and suddenly everything seemed better. Taking his hand again, she laughed and kissed him again, on the lips this time. "We'll be starving by the time dinner's ready."

"Shall I jog back ahead of you and get things started?" he asked, and she made a face.

"No. I want to be with you, and I'm in no condition to jog all those miles."

As a compromise, they walked briskly, holding hands so that their arms were warmly together. They went to bed soon after the dishes were washed, and clung together between the spread sleeping bags. They stayed pressed tightly together all night, turning over almost in unison so that they were never separated for more than a few seconds. They didn't make love, and when Rebecca woke in the night she thought sleepily that somehow the comfort of their warm bodies was greater than if they had been driven by sexual desire.

In the morning she woke up with her head on his shoulder and one arm and one leg flung across him. The sleeping bag had slipped down around their waists, but she felt quite warm. She kissed his neck, and his eyes opened immediately.

"Is it time to get up?" he asked, and she laughed.

"Depends on what you mean by getting up." She kissed his lips, which were surprisingly cool, and pulled him to his side as her legs wrapped around him.

"I see what you mean," he murmured into her ear as their bodies locked, and she sighed, no longer interested in talking.

She moved against him, luxuriously and slowly at first, and then more rapidly as the heat spread and radiated through her body. The only sound was their rapid breathing as she tried to pull him still deeper, wanting to feel him at the very core of her being. Then, quite suddenly, her legs and stomach began to tremble and she arched back in a shuddering climax that unleashed a storm of emotion in her.

"Oh, Jared!" she cried, and tears ran down her face and onto his naked shoulder.

"What is it?" He held her tightly and she burrowed against him, belatedly realizing that their lovemaking had ended before he was satisfied.

She sniffled as delicately as possible. "You didn't have to stop," she said. "I'm fine, really. I just felt very emotional for a few seconds."

His lips moved over her damp cheeks. "I couldn't possibly make love to you while you cry. I care about you too much to ignore the fact that you're unhappy. So you might as well tell me what's really wrong."

"I just don't know if I can stick this out." She shook her head helplessly, wondering how to explain. "I love you so much, and when I feel as if you love me less than that, it hurts me. And I'm afraid it will hurt me so much that I'll have to leave you."

"Like you did before?" His voice was very soft and tender, and she nodded into his chest.

"Like I did before."

He tried to hold her away from him and look at her, but she clung to him, aware that her nose was red and her eyes swollen. "I don't think it's correct to say that you love me more than I love you. I don't think that's the case at all. I'm just not sure right now that love always means forever. I do know I wouldn't want to involve a child in a temporary relationship. I have too much firsthand experience of the effects of doing that."

Rebecca finally pulled away and looked at him, tracing with one finger the lines of worry across his forehead. "Life is temporary," she said. "There are never any guarantees."

Jared sighed, his eyes dark and wounded. "I just don't trust myself yet."

"Do you trust me?" she asked softly, her finger drawing circles on his shoulder.

"I don't know." He pulled her close abruptly, and she put her arms around his neck, pressing her body close against him as if she could draw the pain from his bones. He'd opened himself to her. He was vulnerable, and she would have given anything to help him.

She moved her lips against his chest. "Trust me, please. I love you," she said.

"We'll work things out one way or another," he

whispered into her hair, and somehow they drifted off to sleep in each other's arms.

"We'd better get going! It's a long way from here to San Francisco," Rebecca announced when she opened her eyes and saw how high the sun was. "I'll bet it's after ten!"

Jared groaned. "It may be our last day but we are still on vacation. Where is it written that we have to jump up at the crack of dawn and perform calisthenics?"

"Calisthenics? Is that what you call it?" Rebecca nipped him on the shoulder and jumped up. "Last one in the shower has to disconnect the propane." But all she heard as she hurried down the hall was another groan.

They were on the road by noon, having breakfasted on French toast from the last of the bread and eggs. The sun beat in through the car windows, making Rebecca feel drowsy, and she spent most of the trip home in a half-doze, turning occasionally to watch Jared's profile as he drove.

He was one of the most attractive men she had ever seen. There was nothing pretty about his face, although his features were regular and well matched. A photograph of him, like the one in the newspaper, would reveal nothing but a reasonably good-looking man with a full head of curly hair. It was the gentleness she saw in his eyes, the warmth of his smile, the complete lack of pretense in his facial expressions that made him so appealing to her. And, of course, the fact that she knew him and loved him.

He carried her things into her condominium and deposited them at the foot of the stairs.

"Shall I dredge up some lunch?" Rebecca asked,

thinking of the few dried leftovers that might remain in her refrigerator, and he laughed.

"Sounds delicious, but I want to get back to my place." There was a short silence, and Rebecca felt sure he could hear her heart thumping. "Have you thought about moving in with me? You could bring some things over tonight, if you wanted to."

His face was neutral, his voice calm. Rebecca, on the other hand, felt stirrings of panic in her chest. She loved Jared and she wanted as much of him as she could have. But she hadn't had time to think about giving up her own home and moving to his without his making any promise as to what the future would hold. The idea seemed a little overwhelming. She chose the words of her reply carefully.

"I need a little more time to think about it," she said hesitantly. "I'm not absolutely sure what I want to do."

He scowled. "You mean, whether you want to live with me without benefit of matrimony?"

She gestured to the sofa, but he seemed to prefer standing in the doorway. "Well," she said, "that's one of the things I have to think about."

The color in his face deepened, and she realized with a tiny shock that he was getting angry. "You may think I'm not committed to you, but look at things from my point of view. At least I want you to move in because I value you for yourself and not because I've decided it's time to settle down and raise kids and you just happen to be available."

"I think you've misunderstood me," she said angrily. "It's not just anyone I want, it's you. When we were apart, some people thought I should just shop around for another man. But I didn't, because I knew it was only you I wanted. I wouldn't have been interested in seeing anyone else."

156

She hadn't reassured him, that was obvious. He didn't seem angry anymore, but something was still bothering him. Each time she brought up the weeks they hadn't seen one another, she felt that same tension emanating from him, and suddenly she thought she could guess its source.

"What about you?" she asked in a high, thin voice. "Did you date anyone else?"

"Yes, I had four or five dates," he said, and even though she'd somehow expected it, the blow still hurt.

"Four or five dates?" she echoed. "I thought you said you'd be waiting for my call. How long did you wait? A day? Two days?" She was appalled to hear how shrill her voice had grown, but there was no hope that she could calm down now.

"Don't make a big deal out of this," he said, and she gave a theatrical laugh.

"No, I certainly won't make a big deal out of it. You made it clear that you were fickle, that you couldn't stay with one woman. I just didn't believe you. I thought I knew you better than you knew yourself, that's all." She laughed again, derisively. She couldn't bear to see him standing there, looking hurt and upset, and know that she was the cause. She couldn't bear any of it anymore.

"I want to think about this by myself," she said.

He stepped toward her, his face darkening as she instinctively moved away. "Don't ask me to leave when you're so upset," he said. "I can't just walk away and leave you like this."

"I want you to go," she said, waving her arms as if she could shoo him out the door.

He moved toward her again, holding his hands out to her. It was partly as if he were trying to placate a wild animal, partly as if he wanted to take her in his arms. "Shouldn't we be together when things are difficult?" he asked. "Isn't that the kind of commitment you've been talking about?"

"Maybe so. But right now . . ." She swallowed hard as her voice cracked. "Right now it hurts too much to be with you. I'll call you."

He turned away a little, seemingly resigned. "I thought you'd call last time, too, but you never did."

"I'll call by next Sunday, I promise." She hurried him out the door, as if his absence would solve all her problems.

As soon as the door closed behind him, she locked it and went upstairs to her bedroom, where she kicked off her shoes and crawled under the quilt on her bed. She lay very still, the quilt pulled over her head and her knees drawn up to her chest. It was childish, she knew, but it was her response to pain, and it was one that had served her well. Toothaches, stomachaches, and heartaches all seemed to be quieted by this temporary withdrawal from the world. Now it was the only way to banish images of Jared whispering in some other woman's ear, caressing another woman's body.

Soon the cats jumped on the bed and kneaded comfortable spots for themselves, one against the small of her back and one at her ankles. Their soft purrs soothed her as she lay there and saw, through the filter of the quilt, the daylight fade into evening. Before too long she would have to unpack and get ready for work the next day. She should call Madeleine, too, and thank her for feeding the cats. With a sigh she emerged from her cocoon and stripped off her clothes. First she would take a very long, hot bath in her big tub. Then she would proceed with the rest of her life.

CHAPTER NINE

On Monday night she and Madeleine went out to dinner while Cal baby-sat, and over poppyseed cake Rebecca found herself confiding her troubles, although she felt she could predict Madeleine's advice without asking.

"The thing is," Rebecca said, finding that talking helped her clarify her thoughts, "we've only known each other about six months. And Jared is getting more committed, although very slowly. But the more he gives, the harder I push for an even bigger commitment, and I don't understand why I can't be content with what I have."

Madeleine slowly stirred the remains of her tea. "Maybe you sense that he's afraid of the commitments he's making, that he secretly wants to retract them."

"I think it's just that I'm greedy. I want all of him, forever. I want his children, too, and I don't know if he'll ever change his mind about that."

"There are plenty of other fish in the sea."

Rebecca shook her head, almost laughing. That was just what she'd expected to hear. "But he's the one fish I want."

Madeleine tapped the table impatiently with an extra spoon. "You haven't really looked, you know. Maybe Jared's not the one for you at all."

"Oh, he's the one for me, all right. But I could live

159

without him if I have to, and it may come to that." She hesitated. "He wants me to move in with him."

"I wouldn't do it, unless he's willing to consider marriage and children." Madeleine was unusually brusque. "You'd just be wasting your time."

They paid at the cashier's counter and left. "I never knew you were so hard-hearted until I met Jared," Rebecca said as they climbed into the car.

"A woman has to consider her own best interests," Madeleine said. "The days are gone when women had to drop everything to catch a passing male. I love Cal, but don't think I've ever sacrificed what I wanted for his sake. Our interests have coincided so far, fortunately."

Rebecca found no reply. Madeleine and Cal had always seemed so blissfully happy, so deeply in love, that she'd never thought that either one of them had sat down and weighed the pros and cons of the relationship. It made her wonder if Jared was right about love and she was wrong.

"You know what I think?" Madeleine said as they were stopped at a traffic light. "I think you're like the general who's still fighting the last war. Your experience with Ed made you overreact to anything that reminds you at all of him. Maybe you're afraid that Jared will be unfaithful."

Rebecca shook her head. "I've never heard anyone come down so neatly on both sides of an issue."

"I have that luxury and you don't," Madeleine agreed. "It's your decision to make, after all. And anyway, I've never heard Jared's side of the story."

Neither had she recently, Rebecca realized. Not after she'd found out he'd been dating someone else. Of course he'd had every right to see other women. She'd left, with no promise to come back. But it did seem that he could have allowed a decent interval to elapse

160

before he decided to start looking around. And if he'd really cared for her, surely that would have happened automatically.

"Anyway, why does he want *you* to move in with *him?*" Madeleine asked. "Couldn't he stay at your place just as easily?"

"His place is bigger, it's close to both our jobs, and mine is far away," Rebecca said. "I hadn't really thought about it that concretely, I guess. I don't even know if I could take the cats."

Madeleine squeezed her shoulder. "If you do decide to go, we'll miss you," she said, and Rebecca nodded silently. It really would be a big step, to leave her own place for Jared's.

Later that night she called Alice because she felt obliged to thank her for letting her and Jared use the cabin. She certainly wasn't enthusiastic about telling Alice the outcome of her matchmaking efforts, but of course once Alice asked, she had little choice.

"I hope my absence accomplished all it was intended to," Alice said after reassuring Rebecca that she had had a very nice time in San Diego.

"Only temporarily," Rebecca told her. "We can't seem to keep things together very long."

"I saw the way you two looked at each other down at the lake," Alice said. "I don't think you should let something like that slip out of your grasp."

At least Alice couldn't see her blush over the phone. "I thought I was very careful not to look at Jared at all," she said.

Alice's voice was amused. "Not careful enough. Anyway, if I were you, I'd keep trying. I saw the way he looked at you, too, remember, and for a look like that I'd kill."

Rebecca was noncommittal. "I'll see what I can

do," she said finally. "In the meantime, I'd like to treat you to a very fancy dinner next week."

They fixed a time, and she hung up. It was hard to put Alice's words out of her mind. Rebecca did want Jared, there was no question about that, but somehow she had a hard time trusting him. And not just because of Ed, either. Jared himself had tried to discourage her from putting too much faith in him.

She sat at the table, chin in hand, and tried to think. If a friend came to her for advice in the same situation, what would she recommend? Her mind didn't seem to work. At times like this she almost wished she smoked cigarettes. That way, even when she was just sitting, it would seem as if she were doing something. She twisted a strand of hair between her fingers, then pulled it hard in frustration. She would call Jared as she had promised, that much was certain. And she would continue to see him, as long as he wanted her to. But the idea of moving into his house with the understanding that her presence there would only be temporary—the thought made her palms damp. With a shrug she went upstairs and got ready for bed. She had time still to think about what she would do, and she certainly wasn't getting anywhere sitting there pulling her hair.

When she woke up in the morning her eyes flew open and she thought immediately that Jared might not have had time to think about her moving in. They hadn't really talked about it, and maybe it wasn't something he would want, once he thought it over. So why was she spending energy agonizing over what might prove to be academic? She should call him; they could get together for dinner and talk things out.

But somehow she didn't call him that day or the next. And by Thursday a simple phone call seemed inadequate. What could she say, after making him wait so long, and for the second time? How could she tell him what she wanted, when she was so uncertain herself? She sat over her microwaved dinner and watched the telephone, wondering when she would pick it up. Her indecisiveness was neurotic. The longer she waited, the greater the chance that she would lose him altogether. He had other women on tap, obviously, and he'd probably already called one for a date.

At the thought, something finally crystallized in her mind. At one time she had vowed that where Jared was concerned she would go for broke. So what was she doing picking at a macaroni dinner and dithering over a way to protect her old maid life-style? It was time to prove what she was made of.

With practiced sweetness she called the cats, then stuffed them unceremoniously into their large wire carrier. She ran upstairs and packed a small suitcase with enough clothes to last several days, put a few new journals into her briefcase, swept the contents of her medicine cabinet into a zippered bag, and she was ready. A blare of trumpets wouldn't have seemed out of place as the garage door closed behind her. She was off to find out what her fortune might be.

Jared might not be home, but she had a key. *He might have a woman there,* she thought as she exited from the freeway. If so, the woman would have to go. Rebecca Simpson was not one to slink away in the night in defeat. She narrowed her eyes in preparation for battle. Actually, she reminded herself, turning off the ignition as she glided silently into Jared's driveway, she'd never really enjoyed competition. If he had someone there, she'd try not to run off with her tail between her legs, but she couldn't really expect more than that of herself. Certainly she wasn't about to exchange vinegary remarks with any glamorous visitor.

There didn't seem to be many lights on inside, she

163

noted as she stacked her belongings neatly on the doorstep. It was quite dark, and the sky was starless, making her think it might rain before morning. It would be the first real rain of the season—an ideal night to spend in bed with Jared. She got her umbrella out of the car and laid it on top of her suitcase. The cats were beginning to protest their confinement now that they had been removed from the tortures of the car, and Rebecca knew it was time to knock on the door.

She wondered why the house was so dark. It was only nine-thirty; so Jared was more likely out somewhere than asleep. She raised the knocker and felt her entire body begin to tremble very slightly as she pounded loudly on the strike plate. She waited a minute, her heart leaping in her chest, then banged again.

"I'm coming, for Pete's sake!" came Jared's irritated voice.

The porch light came on, then the door opened to reveal Jared, shirtless and looking somehow unlike himself.

"Here I am," she said unnecessarily as he studied the cat carrier with some bewilderment. "Do you still want me?"

A slow smile spread across his face. "Of course I want you. Why do you think I'm so drunk?"

Rebecca laughed, more from relief than from the non sequitur.

"I didn't know about the cats," she said as he picked up the carrier and pondered its complaining inhabitants. Suddenly she was nervous again. "If you don't want them here, maybe I can find a good home for them. I can't ask Madeleine to keep feeding them." She was babbling, and she closed her mouth quickly.

"Any pet of yours is a pet of mine," Jared said,

opening the carrier in the living room. "I think we have our priorities all wrong, anyway."

"We do?" Rebecca smoothed her hair, steeling herself for a long, serious talk.

"Absolutely. Come here," he said, opening his arms, and she stepped into them gratefully.

He tasted of Scotch, and she smiled to herself. She'd never seen him drink too much before, and certainly he was far from intoxicated now. But his hands were a little clumsy on her back, and his kiss was occasionally too hard.

"I won't make love to you tonight," he said in such a low voice that she could barely hear him. "It wouldn't be right."

"Why not?" she murmured, warming her hands selfishly on the bare skin of his back.

"I'd be clumsy and inconsiderate and then later I'd wish I'd waited. So I'll just spare us all of that." He pulled away to smile at her. "If this is as important an occasion as I think it is, we can celebrate it properly in the morning."

A gust of wind blew into the room and Rebecca shivered. They'd left the front door open, and her belongings were still sitting on the step.

"Let's get you settled in, and then we can have some hot tea," Jared suggested.

"I'd rather just stand here with your arms around me," Rebecca said, snuggling closer to him.

He kissed her cheek and her nose. "You'll be singing a different tune tomorrow, when all your clean clothes are soaking wet and you have to go off to work in the clothes you arrived in." He stepped away and studied her. "You wore that skirt the second time I saw you, and I really liked it." He smiled and shook his head. "I liked everything about you—your hair, your smile, your funny voice."

Rebecca didn't know whether to be pleased or insulted. "I never thought my voice was funny."

"It sounds like you have the tail end of a case of laryngitis," he said with a grin.

"I can see this discussion isn't going to be one I'll want to put in my diary. So let's terminate it and get my things in."

He kissed her soundly. "I love your voice. Any fourteen-year-old boy would give his allowance to have a voice like that."

"You just keep making things worse." Rebecca laughed and pushed him away. "Is this what liquor always does to you?"

"It loosens my tongue." He picked up all her luggage and carried it into the spare bedroom. Rebecca sat down on the bed, chin in hand, and looked up at him.

"For some reason," she said, "I thought we'd be sleeping together."

He turned quickly from the closet, where he was putting her umbrella on the shelf. "We will be. But I thought you'd want your own space, too, with a desk and a chair and so forth. If you don't like the decor, we can change it."

Rebecca looked around thoughtfully. The dominant color in the room was pale green—in stripes on the wallpaper of one wall, in the window curtains and the bedspread. It wasn't her favorite color, and together with the cream-colored carpet and cream-painted walls it made the room quite subdued. On a dark, rainy day like tomorrow would be, the room would be a little chilly-looking.

"Well." She tried to think of the best approach to take. "I like brighter colors, myself. But I think it would be a little precipitous to start redecorating your house."

166

He sat down rather heavily at the desk, swiveling the chair around to face her. "I want you to be happy here. You're not just a weekend guest, you know." He slapped a hand to his forehead, and Rebecca watched him alertly.

"Speaking of weekend guests," he said, "I invited my sister here for the weekend. I was going to take her to the beach, maybe go to the city on Sunday, things like that."

"Of course she'll come," Rebecca said firmly. "Would you like me to spend the weekend at my place?" Somehow things were turning out to be more complicated than she'd anticipated.

"No, no." He hesitated, frowning. "Let's talk about it in the morning, if you don't mind. I think the wisest thing for me to do at this point is to go to bed and sleep this off."

She looked at him critically. He seemed more sober than when he had opened the door. Obviously the shock of her arrival had been bracing for him, and as far as she could tell, he was in good condition. But if he didn't feel up to talking, it was probably best to go along with him.

"Would you like me to sleep in here tonight, since you're not feeling well?"

"No." He pulled her close for a minute. "This hasn't been much of a welcome for you, I know. I won't compound my crime by asking you to sleep alone. We should be together, tonight of all nights."

They walked together to his bedroom, their arms around each other's waist. "I promise not to drown my sorrows in Scotch again," he said, sitting down on the side of the bed and taking off his shoes. "I think the hangover's started already."

"Good," Rebecca said briskly. "Then you'll be a new man in the morning." His state had been rather touching at first, but by now she was a little tired of it. Not that she wanted to sit up all night talking and making plans—after all, she was sleepy too. But she had thought they would make love.

Resolving to be very mature about the situation, she slipped out of her clothes and slid into bed while Jared was still struggling with his socks. By the time he had turned off the light, she was already asleep.

It was still dark when she woke up, her body alive with sensation from the expert brush of Jared's fingertips. She threw the sheet off her burning shoulders and turned to him, groping in the dark to determine his position. She nipped his lower lip with her teeth, then kissed him deeply, pulling him toward her and guiding his hips. She was ready for him. She felt as if she'd been wanting him for weeks.

"Marry me, Diamond," he said huskily, and she clung to him. He was drunk and exhausted and she certainly wouldn't hold him to any promise he made this night. She knew he couldn't have changed his mind so quickly about marriage, but it was very dear of him to want to make her happy. Her eyes were moist as the waves of physical pleasure began to wash over her, and as she murmured his name she knew that she loved him more than ever.

They fell asleep again locked in each other's arms, and when the alarm went off in the morning it seemed to take them several minutes to disentangle themselves enough so that Jared could reach the clock and stop the noise. They smiled at each other and Jared kissed her on what seemed to be his favorite spot—her nose.

"This morning you'll discover all the critical things you forgot to bring."

Rebecca jumped out of bed. "I knew you wouldn't mind if I used your razor and your toothbrush," she said, relishing the look that spread over his face. "And deodorant, too, of course."

"Of course," he said weakly. "What are friends for?"

"Exactly." There was a bathroom off the green bedroom, and she headed in that direction, then turned back and stuck her head through the door. "And could I borrow your blue striped tie to wear as a belt today?"

"Certainly." He lay back in bed as if he'd never get up, and Rebecca smirked a little as she turned on the shower. That would teach him to propose marriage when he didn't really mean it.

They met in the kitchen half an hour later, and Jared looked at her narrowly. "You seem to have managed without borrowing any of my things," he said finally, and she shrugged.

"That was just a test of your love. Actually, I wouldn't consider using your toothbrush."

Jared handed her a cup of coffee. "I don't know whether to be relieved or insulted." He sat down at the table, and they smiled at each other.

"Now, about your sister," Rebecca prompted.

He rubbed at the side of his face with his hand. "I guess I hadn't really thought that through. I like to have her over at least once a week, so there's no chance of disguising the fact that you're here. And I assume you'll be bringing more things than you have right now."

Rebecca nodded. "It might not be good for your sister, you know. She may see me as competition and feel as if she's lost you."

"Then she'll have to learn how to cope. I'm not having you slink around or feel guilty because you've disconcerted my sister. I'll talk it over with her when I pick her up, and I'm sure we'll be able to work things out." He pushed his chair back and stood up. "What would you like for breakfast?"

Rebecca glanced at her watch. "I'd better slug my coffee and go, as soon as I feed the cats. Where *are* the cats?"

"You forgot cat food, so I gave them a can of tuna and they're now sleeping it off on the living room windowsill."

Rebecca shook her head. "I can't believe I forgot cat food. I'll have to get organized this weekend." She walked up behind him as he spread butter on an English muffin, and kissed the back of his neck. " 'Bye." He turned and curved his arms around her back.

"I need a better good-bye than that," he said, one hand stroking her hair back from her face. "Let's not start acting like an old married couple so early in our relationship."

She swayed against him as their lips met softly and moved together. His mustache was very bristly, and she wrinkled her nose a little at the sensation against her upper lip. He pressed her buttocks against him and she pulled away, laughing.

"Why is your mustache so sharp today?" she asked, rubbing her lip.

"I trimmed it yesterday." He stroked it with the top of his forefinger. "Did it scratch you?"

"No." She leaned forward to kiss him again, one hand in the shower-damp curls of his hair. The morning had been too short. With an exaggerated sigh she rested her head against his shoulder. "If I don't leave now, I'll be late."

"Grab your raincoat and I'll walk you to the car," he said, and she smiled as she went back down the hall.

"Is it raining? I never even noticed."

"No, it's not now, but it's bound to soon."

The cloud cover was very heavy, she saw as they walked to the car, and the air was damp and surprisingly warm. But not even a drop of rain had fallen—the thin layer of dust on her car was unmarred. Her clothes, chosen for colder weather, already seemed sticky and heavy. She and Jared embraced at the car, lingering for a moment, and then she gave him a final, solid kiss and he opened the car door for her.

"When's your birthday?" he asked, and she froze.

"It's today!"

"Well, happy birthday." He kissed her again, several tiny kisses around the edges of her lips, until she shook her head.

"Now I really will be late." She settled herself quickly in the car and drove off, glancing in the rearview mirror to see him walking back to the house. She drove as quickly as she could through the morning traffic, impatient to be at work. Still there was time to wonder how she had forgotten her birthday when it had been looming so large in her thoughts. Was it because she didn't want to be thirty, or had the reunion with Jared really taken up so much of her attention that she had put her birthday out of her mind?

No one forgets her own birthday, she decided as she parked her car and headed for the elevator. Especially not her thirtieth birthday. She met her first patients in the elevator going up, and she shrugged the matter of her failing memory aside. There were more important things to attend to now.

She had an unusually full schedule that day and left the office at eight, having had a quick hamburger for dinner. It was good to see the lights on when she arrived at Jared's house, and she reminded herself that for now, at least, his house was her home. She'd be coming here every evening whether Jared was home or not, helping with the cooking and cleaning and gardening, no longer a guest. It seemed strange.

The cats were at the door when she opened it, and she had to push them back inside.

"Maybe in a few weeks you can go outside," she told them, bending over to stroke their thick fur, and when she looked up Jared was there, holding two glasses of champagne.

"I thought you wouldn't want a full-scale celebration tonight, since it's so late, but we can still live it up a little."

He led her into the dining room, where she saw a chocolate cake resting beautifully on a crystal plate. Next to it stood three tall, very thin candles in a gracefully curving silver candelabra. The table was set with a white linen tablecloth, crystal dessert plates, and gleaming silver forks. At the far end of the table stood a silver vase filled with fresh red roses, next to a square package wrapped in shiny, thick blue paper and tied with a silver ribbon.

"You've been very busy," she said, kissing him on the cheek. "It's all so beautiful. Where did you get that wonderful cake?"

"Get?" He drew himself up and scowled at her. "You think I would have you eat store-bought birthday cake?"

She sat down and looked at the cake more closely. "You made that? How did you find the time?"

He smiled a little, picking up the cake server to cut a thick slice gleaming with icing. "I took the afternoon off."

The scent of roses filled her nostrils, and her eyes felt a little moist as she took her first bite of cake. She'd never known that a man could be so thoughtful. It made her almost shy to think that Jared had worked so hard to create a nice birthday for her.

"Are you going to open your present?" he asked, watching her fondly as her tongue chased a cake crumb at the corner of her mouth. Maybe he should have bought her a diamond ring, he thought. It had seemed presumptuous, especially since she hadn't responded to his proposal of marriage.

And why hadn't she? He'd wondered about it all day, unsure if perhaps she just hadn't heard him. More likely she was having second thoughts after arriving and finding him drunk. She might suspect him of being a secret drinker. Or she might just want more time to be sure. Now that he'd told her he wanted to marry her, he wasn't going to push her. When she was ready, she'd no doubt let him know.

Rebecca opened the package slowly. She'd always felt obliged to preserve wrapping paper if at all possible. In fact, she had a drawer full of carefully folded paper that of course she never reused. Putting the paper and ribbon aside, she lifted the lid of the box to reveal a nightgown of pale gold silk, cut low in the front and back and slit up the sides.

"Shall I try it on?" she asked, looking up at him through her lashes.

"Absolutely." He took another bite of cake.

She retired to her room with the box and changed, admiring herself in the full-length mirror before she went back out to Jared. The gown had what she thought of as a Greek bodice, with shoulder straps that formed a V between her breasts and crossed underneath them. It was a flattering style, lifting her breasts a little and making them seem fuller.

The color was perfect for her, accenting her tan and lightening her eyes to amber, and the fabric was opaque enough to add a little mystery to her body. The gown reached her feet and was perfectly straight and slit to the middle of the thigh on each side. As she moved, the silk parted to reveal glimpses of her legs, which appeared even more long and slender than they were. It was lovely.

She walked back to the dining room, wishing she had some little gold high-heeled slippers to wear, and Jared's face lit up when he saw her. He stood immediately and walked across the room to her, where he ran his hands slowly up and down her bare arms.

"I did an excellent job of selection," he said huskily, and gave her a long kiss that banished all thoughts of chocolate cake from her mind. "Of course," he said, pulling away just enough to allow his mustache to tickle her lip, "I had to hug every saleswoman in the store before I found one that seemed to be your size."

"You did not," she replied happily, putting a little pressure on the back of his head to bring his lips to hers. She hadn't always trusted him, but for tonight at least she was confident of his interest in her and her alone.

Their lips and hands moved in a leisurely exploration, and Rebecca sighed deeply, stroking his wonderful curly hair. Without speaking they turned and went arm and arm into the bedroom. She felt very warm, very ready, as Jared threw back the covers and bent to lift her new gown slowly up from her ankles and over her head. She lay down on the cool sheets and watched him undress, a faint smile on her lips.

She already knew how good it would be, and she murmured happily as his lips touched the hollow of her neck, the rounded sides of her breasts, and then her own lips. They made love slowly and sweetly, in a tender union that seemed never to end. She was aware of his body as she had never been before—every ridge, every pulsating vein became so familiar to her that she could hardly tell his body from her own.

They lay quietly afterward for several minutes, until

Rebecca began stroking his chest with the tip of one finger. He leaned over and kissed her on the cheek. "Shall we get up or stay in bed?" he asked, and she sat up immediately.

"I hardly even tasted my cake," she said, outraged. "I'm certainly not going to bed yet."

"Very well." He stood and rummaged in the closet. "Do you want my maroon robe or my orange one?"

She giggled. "Don't you have a chartreuse one? Or canary yellow?"

"These were gifts from my sister," he said with great dignity. "She used to like bright colors."

Rebecca held out her hand for the orange robe. "Speaking of your sister," she said, belting the robe around her waist, "we'd better decide what to do."

Jared sighed as they walked to the table. "I've worried about being a bad influence on her, but I do have to live my own life. I've decided that the most important thing is to tell her the truth. I'll spend the day with her tomorrow, then bring her back here for dinner. And maybe the three of us can spend Sunday together."

"Do you think she'll want to do that?"

Jared seemed startled. "You'll be like the big sister she never had. I'm sure she'll love you just the way I do."

Rebecca was silent. In Meredith's place, she wouldn't welcome the unexpected intrusion of a strange woman into her relationship with her brother. It would only be natural for Meredith to dislike Rebecca on sight, but with any luck she'd be polite, at least at the beginning.

All day Saturday Rebecca felt a little prickle of worry about meeting Jared's sister. Driving back and forth to work, and later on the way to her condominium to pick up more of her things, she tried to prepare herself to make everything go as smoothly as possible. It would be very important to Jared that the two of them get along. In fact, it was essential to all three of them, since they would probably be spending a fair amount of time together over the next months. She hoped her appearance on the scene wouldn't be too much for Meredith to handle.

She put her mail in her car and then, after some thought, went to an electronics store and bought a telephone answering machine that would allow her to pick up her messages from Jared's house. She wasn't ready yet to change her telephone number to his. She left a note promising to call Madeleine, who was out. She turned off the pilot light to the water heater and, with a last check of the doors and windows, got back into her car.

She didn't say good-bye in her mind. All her furniture, dishes, and linens were still there, all her books and journals. She could move back any day she wanted, since she hadn't really moved in with Jared. The refrigerator still had to be cleaned out, she realized as she drove down the freeway. That would have to be done later in the week.

It was after four by the time she had unloaded her car at Jared's, and she expected him and Meredith to arrive at any moment. When the Volvo pulled into the driveway a little before five, she took a very deep breath and sat down in the living room.

Jared came in and introduced his sister, who was prettier than Rebecca had expected. Certainly she was thin, but not dangerously so. Her features had been a little sharpened by weight loss, and the calves beneath her plaid skirt were barely rounded, but Rebecca had seen many girls who were much thinner, with legs like toothpicks and huge, hollow eyes. She was relieved to see that Meredith appeared to be in no immediate danger.

"How did she take the news?" Rebecca asked as soon as Meredith had disappeared down the hall to unpack.

Jared shrugged. "She wasn't excited, I guess, but I think she'll be okay. I told her we'd go out for pizza tonight, if you agreed."

"Sure." Even if she hated pizza, she wouldn't have said so now.

Meredith came out a few minutes later dressed in brand-new jeans and a pink blouse, and Rebecca met her rather icy look with her best smile.

"We'd better take an umbrella," she said. "I'm still expecting rain."

"The weatherman said the clouds would blow over," Meredith countered immediately.

"It won't hurt to take an umbrella along, just in case," Jared said, reaching into the closet, as Meredith pouted.

"I *told* you, it's not going to rain."

Rebecca's smile began to feel a little thin. "Since Meredith has listened to the forecast, we won't need to bother with the umbrella, I guess."

Jared closed the door a little irritably. "Let's go, then," he said, and they went.

At the pizza parlor Meredith insisted on having anchovies on the pizza and then picked languidly at one narrow slice while Jared used visible self-control to avoid urging her to eat. Rebecca gave up her dogged cheerfulness and ate silently, grimacing a little each time she bit into an anchovy. It was a long and silent meal.

Back at Jared's, Meredith turned on the television and sat on the floor in front of it, ostentatiously engrossed in a rerun of an old comedy show. Jared shrugged helplessly and went into the kitchen, where Rebecca joined him.

"Things will get better," she said. "This probably happened a little too quickly for her, and she's at an awkward age anyway."

"But she's always been so sweet," Jared said, rubbing his temples. "I don't recognize this side of her at all."

Rebecca sat down on the bench beside the kitchen table. "Objectively speaking, it wasn't really that bad. After all, it didn't rain. And we should have put at least one foot down about the anchovies, so that was our fault." She smiled. "In some ways it was rather funny."

"It's easy for you to be so relaxed about it. She's not *your* sister."

Rebecca was a little stung, but she didn't show it. She knew she wasn't foolish enough to let Meredith's behavior lead her into an argument with Jared. "I hope to get much better acquainted with her," she said after a little thought. "But for now I think I'll retire to the bedroom and read for a while. Maybe she'd like some more time alone with you."

Jared sighed. "I'll give it a try, anyway."

He came to bed quite late, after Rebecca had already put her book down and turned out the light, and she stroked his arm sleepily when she felt him next to her. "Everything okay?" she asked, and he was silent for a minute.

"I guess so," he answered finally, and she went back to sleep.

She woke up several hours later as a flash of lightning illuminated the room. There was a rumble of thunder, not too close by, and then she heard a faint sound like one of the cats crying. Rebecca tried to think. She knew she hadn't seen the cats since

178

Meredith's arrival, but she'd assumed they were curled up in their favorite spot near the heating vent in Jared's study.

After another flash and its following thunder, the sound came again and she slipped out of bed. The cats might be outside in the rain, or shut up in a room somewhere ready to wreak havoc. She slipped on the orange robe and padded out into the hall, closing the bedroom door very softly behind her.

The living room, frequently illuminated by flashes of lightning, was unoccupied; neither were any soaked cats clinging to the outside windowsills. All was well in the kitchen, so Rebecca turned back and walked down the hall to the study. The cats were there, wide awake, and followed her as she wandered back to the middle of the hall and stood undecided.

There was a clap of thunder loud enough to make her jump, and the sound came again, from Meredith's room. Squaring her shoulders, she tapped on the bedroom door, then opened it slowly. Meredith was sitting up in bed, her face ashen and a pillow clutched to her chest. Adrenaline made Rebecca's heart pound.

"Are you okay?" she asked, walking over to the bed. She touched Meredith's forehead briefly and found it quite cool.

"I can't sleep with all this thunder," Meredith said in a small voice, and Rebecca felt all her muscles relax in relief. "I've never seen a storm like this," the girl added, wincing at a rather distant roll of thunder.

"It woke me up too," Rebecca said. The cats had followed her into Meredith's room and began exploring the new territory.

Meredith slid out of bed, looking very young in a pair of pink flannel pajamas. She approached the cats, seeing them for the first time. "Are they yours? Can I pet them?" she asked, sitting on the carpet.

"Yes to both questions," Rebecca said. "If you like, they'll sleep on your bed tonight and keep you company."

Meredith seemed to recover a little of her earlier dislike of Rebecca, a sign that she was feeling less frightened. "Actually, I like dogs better." She frowned. "That's my brother's robe."

"He's letting me borrow it for a few days, until I get one of my own. I hope I can find one this nice."

Meredith nodded. "I chose it." She got back into bed. "Will they really sleep with me?"

Rebecca said yes, hoping she was right. She patted the bed invitingly, and both cats, who were only rarely allowed to sleep with her, jumped up with alacrity and began searching for cozy spots to sleep. "Better leave the door open a little, just in case," she told Meredith. "And if they keep you awake, toss them out." She noticed that the storm seemed to have diminished considerably. "Good night."

"Night."

Rebecca went back to Jared's room. At least now she had the first beginnings of a relationship with Meredith, thanks to the cats. Perhaps Sunday wouldn't be quite as unpleasant as she had feared. She knew that she and Meredith still had a long way to go, but now it seemed possible that at some time they could become friends. That would be very important to Jared, whose loyalty to Meredith was particularly fierce, since he knew she was having problems.

Rebecca slipped carefully between the sheets, and Jared didn't stir. With time, maybe things would come around. Who could say? Maybe the day would come when Jared would really want to marry her as much as she wanted to marry him.

CHAPTER TEN

As the weeks went by, Meredith seemed to have accepted Rebecca, if she still didn't welcome her. Rebecca often made trips to the city, to change the cassette on her answering machine, to pick up her mail, and to bring one or two more items to Jared's house. She tried to schedule many of the trips to coincide with Meredith's visits, so that Jared and his sister could have time alone together. Meredith, however, began bringing a girlfriend, Julie, with her on her visits, and became much less interested in being alone with Jared. Jared was clearly very pleased at this sign that his sister was getting better.

For her part, Rebecca was happy in a way she'd never been before—happy knowing that she would see Jared that night, that she would sleep in his arms. Their lovemaking was still exciting, something that each time left her astonished and grateful that such experiences were possible for her. But each time she visited her condominium, she was reminded that in some ways she was only a guest in Jared's home. She thought about bringing a few more of her things to Jared's, but she knew that would only be a superficial solution to the problem, which was the temporary nature of their relationship.

As if he sensed her feelings, Jared began asking if she didn't want to redecorate, or at least move in some of her own furniture. "We could make the green room into a study for you, or a sort of sitting room, if you like. And if you'd like to bring any of your living room furniture, or your paintings, I'd be delighted."

Rebecca tried to picture a moving van in the driveway, her desk and filing cabinet being wheeled into the house, and she knew something was wrong. "That would be rather permanent, wouldn't it?" she said slowly, and Jared nodded.

"Yes, it would mean that you're not just camping out here for a few months."

She looked at him, and his face was serious. She saw now very clearly what was bothering her, but she wasn't ready to bring things to a head with Jared. "I'd better think it over," she said, and he nodded as if that had been what he expected.

She was living like a gypsy, she told herself later as she sat at the little desk in the green bedroom. No wonder she felt sad when she visited her old home. Now she was in limbo, and it wasn't a matter of furniture or tapestries. It was a matter of commitment. She was afraid to move in too many of her things, afraid that she'd start feeling too secure. She couldn't afford to forget that Jared didn't believe in permanence or lifelong commitments. She needed to hold a small part of herself in reserve, ready for the day she would have to leave. And when that day came, she wanted to be able to load her things into the Peugeot and go, without having to arrange for packers and a moving van.

This time with Jared was so precious to her, she was afraid to talk with him about her wish for a different state of affairs. There was tension in her, deeply hidden beneath the surface, and a confrontation with him might cause her to lose control. She didn't want to quarrel with him again, and she felt sure their relationship wouldn't survive another rupture caused by the same problem. So she lectured herself every morning and evening. *Be happy. Give what you can and take what you can and don't worry about tomorrow.*

For Thanksgiving Jared and Rebecca invited a number of single people they knew and they worked late into the night on Wednesday making pies and stuffing and breads. The smell of the turkey cooking on Thursday evoked memories of home for Rebecca, times when her mother was alive and the four of them were together as a family. She wanted a family of her own, children who looked like Jared sitting at the Thanksgiving table.

Once the guests began to arrive, she was fully occupied with remembering names and making sure everyone had enough to eat and drink, and she quickly entered into the spirit of the holiday. Alice Fairweather came, bringing a big fruit salad, and seemed delighted to see Jared and Rebecca together. "What did I tell you!" she whispered when she found Rebecca alone in the kitchen, and Rebecca smiled. She had wondered at times if she and Jared would have found each other again without Alice's intervention, and she had decided that was a question they'd never be able to answer. She was doubly grateful to Alice for what she was doing for Jared's sister, and Rebecca was glad Alice hadn't felt she had to refuse their Thanksgiving invitation because of her professional relationship with Jared's family.

To Rebecca's delight, the disparate mix of psychologists, computer scientists, and software salespeople seemed to blend well. By the time they had finished dinner and moved into the living room for coffee and dessert, everyone seemed to be well acquainted and the buzz of conversation never diminished. Rebecca was particularly pleased to see that Alice was usually surrounded by three or four men, all of whom seemed to listen attentively to her every word. Maybe Alice would fall in love at their party. After all, one good turn deserved another.

"It was fun," Rebecca told Jared as the last person left, long after midnight.

"Yes," he answered, putting his arms around her so that she could lean against him, "our friends get along just as well as we do. It's a good sign."

A good sign for what? she wondered. It was as if Jared was thinking about a future for them, but she refused to let herself hope.

It was time to begin shopping for Christmas, and again Rebecca felt the same nostalgia she had around Thanksgiving. Holidays were a time to be in a family, to have children. She wasn't happy in an open-ended relationship, and she could no longer hide it from herself. She wanted to be married to Jared, or at least engaged to him. She wanted to move in lock, stock, and barrel, instead of feeling like a houseguest who had overstayed her welcome. She was back in the same old dilemma again.

For Christmas she bought Jared a new light blue running suit, a set of six silver-inlaid antique wineglasses, and a new book he'd been wanting to read. After Jared held lengthy consultations with his parents, she bought Meredith a gift certificate at a local pet store that would enable her to pick out a kitten after the holidays. Because a gift certificate seemed rather unexciting, she also bought her a new sweater and a frilly nightgown. That shopping done, she found several new shirts for her brother, a velour bathrobe for her stepmother, and a pair of binoculars for her father, who'd become interested in birds.

By the week before Christmas she'd finished wrapping everything, and in a final frenzy of activity she baked several batches of only slightly burned cookies before she flew down to see her family. Her brother was spending Christmas at home, so she planned to spend four days with them, then return just before Christmas.

"Can't I come?" Jared asked a little plaintively.

"The truth is, I've never even mentioned you, so I'm afraid you'd come as something of a shock." Rebecca was embarrassed to realize how secretive she'd been about Jared, although the temporary nature of their living arrangement certainly justified some reticence where her father was concerned.

"You mean, they don't even know you're living here?" he asked.

"They know I'm staying here with a friend, but they don't know it's you, and I doubt they suspect a romance." She looked away and began toying with a newspaper. "I won't be gone long," she said finally.

"I know."

He wasn't satisfied. She'd met all his family by now, although only Meredith knew her well, so she could hardly tell Jared that she was not behaving any differently than he. But she didn't want to take him to Bakersfield and have her father begin plans to attend her wedding, only to have to tell him later that it was over. She wanted to keep her pride intact if she possibly could. She and Jared would have to have a talk after the holidays. But not now.

He drove her to the airport, and she was surprised at the pain she felt in saying good-bye. "I won't be gone long," she said again, as much to herself as to him, and she clung to him until the last possible moment before she boarded the plane.

Her father, although grayer than the last time she had seen him, seemed to be happy and in good health.

Her brother, though he was only eighteen, was considerably more debonair than the skinny high school graduate she had kissed good-bye in September. She and her brother went to movies, played tennis, and visited old friends together, and Rebecca enjoyed his company immensely. As ever, she and her father and stepmother had little to say to one another, but still they were all fond of each other, and their times together were pleasant.

Despite all that, Rebecca impatiently waited for her return to Jared. She fastened her seat belt in the airplane with a light heart, her fingers nearly trembling with excitement and anticipation. However imperfect and impermanent her affair with Jared was, it remained the center of her emotional life. Her previous dissatisfactions seemed unimportant, and she told herself that she would absolutely not try to change Jared's views on marriage, that she would love him and stay with him on whatever terms he wanted.

She rushed into his arms at the airport, delighting in the familiar closeness, and held his arm tightly to her side while they waited for her suitcase. His mood was a little odd, happy but also more tense than usual, and she wondered if his sister was worse, or if he was having problems at work. His kisses were a little brisker than she would have liked, and her elation at returning began to ebb.

He was very quiet on the drive to his house, and her chatter about her trip gradually dwindled to silence as she frowned at his profile. Something was definitely wrong.

"I'm glad you're back," he said as he turned off the freeway, and she relaxed a little. "It seemed as if you were gone for a long time."

"I know, but it was only a few days," she said, putting a tentative hand on his thigh. "I missed you too."

186

"I guess the time seemed longer because there's something I need to say to you. I've been going over it and over it in my mind, getting more and more impatient. Tonight we have to have a serious talk, as soon as we get to my house."

She put her hand back in her lap. This was not at all the homecoming she had envisioned, and it sounded as if things were going to get worse. She tried to prepare herself, imagining various conversations they might have. Maybe he had decided it was time for her to move out. Maybe he thought he was setting a bad example for Meredith. Had he met someone new while she was gone? It hardly seemed possible in such a short time, but then he was a very attractive man.

By the time he had parked the car, her teeth were clenched with worry. He opened the car door and she slid out, waiting impatiently for him to get her suitcase out of the trunk. All she wanted to do was get things out into the open so she would know the worst. She unlocked the front door for him and opened it, only to find her way barred by a golden cord.

"What's this?" she asked, and Jared shrugged.

"You're supposed to follow the cord," he said, handing her the end of the cord, which had been fastened to the doorjamb.

"Did you do this?" she asked, unable to figure out what was happening.

"I did." There seemed to be a smile twitching at one side of his mouth.

She cleared her throat nervously, following the cord around sofas, chairs, and lamps.

"You've reached the end," he said as the cord dove under a sofa cushion, and her hand encountered a very small velvet-covered box.

"Is it—is it what I think?" she asked, and her voice

broke on the last word as she wondered if it was all some terrible joke.

"Open it and see," he said as she held the small blue box in her hand. His voice and smile were very gentle, and suddenly she knew that it would be all right.

It was a diamond ring—in fact, a band of diamonds with one larger stone at the center. It sparkled beautifully in the light as she held it up.

"Look inside," he said, and she read the inscription.

"Tomorrow and always." She threw her arms around his neck, accidentally dropping the ring.

"Oh, Jared," she told him, half laughing and half crying, "it's beautiful, but you could have just asked me, you know."

"I did," he murmured into her hair, "but you didn't answer."

"You were drunk that night," she protested, pulling away. "You didn't know what you were saying."

"Oh, no?" He pulled her close again. "Anyway, this time I decided to ask in a way you couldn't ignore." He kissed her ear.

"Where's my ring?" Rebecca said suddenly, realizing that she had let it fall.

"Where's my answer?" he countered, refusing to let her go.

"Your answer is yes," she said throatily. "And the sooner the better." She ran her fingers softly down the back of his neck. Morning would be soon enough to find the ring. "Tomorrow and always," she added, remembering the inscription, and she kissed him thoroughly.

Candlelight Ecstasy Romances™

$1.95 each